CW01521731

all
about
eve

NEW YORK TIMES BESTSELLING AUTHOR

LILIANA
HART

Copyright © 2010 Liliana Hart

All rights reserved.

ISBN: 1469924692
ISBN-13: 978-1469924694

other single titles
by liliana hart

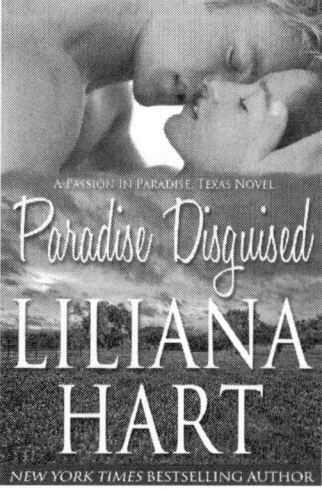

contents

other titles by liliana hart

The MacKenzie Series

Dane
A Christmas Wish: Dane
Thomas
To Catch A Cupid:
Thomas
Riley
Fireworks: Riley
Cooper
A MacKenzie Christmas
Cade
Shadows and Silk
Secrets and Satin
Sins and Scarlet Lace
Sizzle
Crave

The Collective Series

Kill Shot

The Rena Drake Series

Breath of Fire

Addison Holmes Mysteries

Whiskey Rebellion
Whiskey Sour
Whiskey For Breakfast
Whiskey, You're The
Devil

JJ Graves Mysteries

Dirty Little Secrets
A Dirty Shame
Dirty Rotten Scoundrel
Down and Dirty

Standalone Novels/Novellas

All About Eve
Paradise Disguised
Catch Me If You Can
Who's Riding Red?
Goldilocks and the
Three Behrs
Strangers in the Night
Naughty or Nice

chapter one

"*D*evastated in Denver*, you're on the air with Dr. Lovegood. What's on your mind tonight?"

The silky voice floated across the airwaves as gentle as a caress between lovers. It was a voice that inspired sympathy, hope, and in some, lust induced dreams.

Eve Lovegood adjusted her headphones and propped her feet up on the console that held an assortment of jelly donuts and granola bars. No one had made a dent in the granola bars yet, and she knew they'd been there since the four AM morning shift. In fact, they could have been the same granola bars that had been there since she started working at the station three years ago.

She shivered, glad she hadn't been desperate enough to fall off the wagon and gorge herself with a plateful of fried lard or furry granola, and waited for the caller to ask her question. There wasn't time in her hectic schedule to lose another twenty pounds.

"Thanks for taking my call, Dr. Lovegood." The clogged caller had obviously been crying, the sniffles and occasional hiccup giving her away. "I think my husband is having an affair." The woman burst into a fresh round of sobs, and Eve had to spend a few minutes quieting her down enough to listen.

"Have you asked him if he's having an affair?" Eve asked

"Oh, no. I could never do that. What if he leaves me?"

Eve pushed aside her impatience. She had no tolerance for women that stood around and refused to fight for love. It was too precious and much too rare in her mind to throw away just because being a coward was easier. She pushed her own failure out of her mind and focused on *Devastated in Denver*.

"Why do you think your husband is having an affair?" Eve asked gently, trying to smooth the woman's ruffled feathers.

"Because he never wants to make love any more. He just comes home from work, eats the food I put in front of him and then falls asleep in bed watching a movie. It's the same thing every night, even on the weekends."

"Have you tried getting his attention? Maybe greeting him in sexy lingerie or getting him to watch an adult video with you when he lies down at night?"

"Goodness, no," the woman said, scandalized.

Which was, in Eve's opinion, the crux of the problem. People weren't willing to take enough chances when their relationship was on the line.

"What does your husband do, and how long have you been married?"

"He's an OB/GYN, and we're going on eight years."

"Have you ever thought that maybe your husband needs something more than clinical sex in his life with you at home? He looks at a part of the female anatomy dozens of times a day that most men only see when they're involved in intercourse with their partner."

"I've never thought about it that way before," the woman said, as if a light bulb went on above her head. "What should I do?"

"You need to find new ways to make your vagina different than everyone else's. I don't mean that in the physical sense obviously, but your husband needs to see you in a new light. He works long hours and probably doesn't get a lot of time off, so every moment you spend with him needs to count. Instead of watching an adult video together in the evenings, why don't you make a video of yourself so he's surprised when he hits play on the remote? And when you're finished seducing him, tell him your fears about him having an affair or losing interest. He's part of your relationship too, and you should share each other's burdens."

"Thanks, Dr. Lovegood. I'm going to do it tonight. I don't know what I would have done without you." The woman's tears had dried up and a sliver of hope was now in her voice. That hope was what Eve lived for—to know that she'd helped in some way, no matter how small.

"Thank you, *Devastated in Denver*. Please let us know how things work out. You've been listening to Dr. Eve Lovegood on WKTP's national radio syndicate. This is Dr. Lovegood signing out until tomorrow night."

Eve removed her headset and tried to straighten her haphazard ponytail. Her hair had a mind of its own, thick and rich, the true blue black of the Irish and all the unruliness of Little Orphan Annie. She went to great lengths at the beginning of the day to straighten and smooth, but in the end she always ended up with a ponytail that looked like it had been set with TNT.

"Great show tonight, Eve."

"Thanks, Lucy."

Lucy Potter was the producer for Eve's show and her good friend. Everyone around the station called Lucy the *Destroyer*. She was barely an inch over five feet tall, and she could cut a person off at the knees with her sharp tongue if something went wrong during one of her shows. Her dark, corkscrew hair and bright blue eyes didn't soften the blow any because it was like being scolded by Shirley Temple with fangs. Eve adored her. And she secretly admired the way Lucy wore leopard print spandex on a size fourteen frame with no doubts or self-consciousness at all.

"How's Suzanne?" Eve asked, stretching her sore muscles after sitting in a chair for four hours. She bent over and touched her fingers flat to the floor, inciting a wolf whistle from someone walking by the glass enclosed booth that she called her office for a few hours every night. Whoever the whistler was, their love life was sadly lacking if they found a woman in grey sweats and high tops sexy. Eve was glad to be out of private practice just because she never had to wear pantyhose again if she didn't want to. She had the perfect job.

"Suzanne's fine. We're still looking for a house that both of us can agree on. You'd think it would be much easier for two women to buy a house rather than a man and a woman. We both know exactly what we want and we both have a vision.

The problem is that our vision is completely different. Sometimes I think being a lesbian is much harder than when I was married."

Eve smiled sympathetically. "You'll find something. You and Suzanne are a great couple. You'll compromise and both get exactly what you want. Don't worry, house hunting takes time. Look how long it took me to find my house."

"That's true," Lucy said with a sparkle in her eye. "And it looks like you should have taken your own advice, because your house is a disaster. Have you gotten the back porch fixed yet?"

Eve gave Lucy an irritated look for mentioning her poor judgment and started gathering her things. Her back porch had collapsed from the rotted wood that was apparently prominent throughout her entire house. Unfortunately, she'd been standing on it at the time and fallen through to the basement. She tried to look at it as fate lending a helping hand, because she hadn't even realized she'd had a basement. It had been sealed up years before. Her knee was still stiff from the fall.

"No, I've had to put off my plans for the porch. My toilet fell through the floor from the second story last night, so I've moved my list of priorities around a little."

Lucy gasped in horror. "Eve Lovegood, it is *not* safe for you to live in that house until everything is up to code. You could be seriously hurt. What if that toilet had fallen on your head? You can't give advice on people's love lives from six feet under. I'm going to report you to the city inspector myself if you don't get something done about it fast."

And she would, too, Eve knew. Lucy didn't make idle threats. "I'll get it taken care of," Eve said, dutifully scolded. "But I may end up a pauper before I'm done. I didn't realize how much money is going to have to go into this project."

"You couldn't be a pauper in your wildest dreams. You have more money than God."

"Yeah, but this house is going to change my life drastically. I can feel it in my bones. Not to mention the fact that I'm still researching restoration companies and contractors. That's not a decision you can make on the spur of the moment."

"You bought that monstrosity on the spur of the moment, so I think hiring a contractor is small potatoes compared to that. You're going to have to buy life insurance for every person that steps foot on your front porch. That hasn't collapsed yet, has it?"

"No, not yet."

"Well, it's only a matter of time," Lucy said, with confidence.

"You're not helping. I obviously can't take

advice from myself. I don't know how thousands of other people do it. I have rotten judgment. Why don't you give me advice tonight? I'll do whatever you say."

Lucy opened her mouth, but Eve interrupted her before the words could be spoken. "I'll do anything except sell or live somewhere else."

Lucy shot her a dirty look and left the control booth to head back to her desk, her black stilettos clicking against the hard floor. *Friends. . .what a pain.* Eve slung her bag over her shoulder and left the booth, already dreading the night ahead. She was currently sleeping in the middle of the living room because that seemed like the safest place. But she was thinking about setting up a tent in the back yard after the latest bathroom incident.

"Hah, I found it," Lucy said victoriously, waving a business card in the air.

Eve realized that Lucy had taken her seriously when she told her to give the advice for a change. A sinking feeling in her gut made her future seem more than grim. She wasn't good at taking other people's advice. That's why she was always giving it out.

"This is the number of the contractor that did all of the work on our condo last month. He was brilliant. He increased the value of the house a lot, and we've already had several offers from interested buyers. I want you to call and leave a message on his machine tonight," Lucy said, obviously looking for an argument and waiting to combat it.

Eve looked at the card in her hand and back at Lucy. "Hand me the phone." She knew good advice when she heard it.

The company was called Murphy-Madsen Construction and Restoration, and the names of George Madsen and Jake Murphy each occupied a bottom corner of the card in bold print. She decided to go with George because that was a name that said dependable construction in her mind.

The phone rang several times before the answering machine picked up and a gruff voice welcomed her to leave a message and contact information. She smiled at the voice. That had to be George.

"Mr. Madsen, my name is Eve Lovegood, and I'm having a little bit of a construction crisis. You came recommended from a friend, and I'm pretty desperate since the toilet from the second floor bathroom fell into my downstairs bedroom." She left her address and phone number and prayed they would have time in their schedule to help her.

"See, that wasn't so bad," Lucy said, beaming as if she were a proud parent. "You did good, Lovegood."

"Thanks, boss. I'll see you tomorrow night."

"I'm looking forward to it. All the crazies call on Friday night, plus it's a full moon."

Eve groaned at the thought. Friday nights were always interesting.

"Look on the bright side. Somewhere in Denver tonight, a lonely housewife is trying to make her vagina different. Sage advice, Dr. Lovegood," Lucy said, giggling. "That is definitely one for the record books."

"Well, at least someone is getting lucky. Lord knows it's not me."

"That's because every man you might consider for a relationship is going to be terrified of your house."

Eve waved bye to Lucy's delighted laughter and headed down the elevator to the parking garage. Lucy was wrong. Men weren't afraid of her house, they were afraid of her. No one wanted to be with someone who was supposed to be an expert on relationships. Her own failed marriage had taught her that. Good men didn't stay interested in a woman like her after the initial curiosity began to fade. She would have been just another statistic if her divorce from Steve had been finalized before he'd died.

Eve wished she had the luxury of calling in to her own show, because *Lonely in Dallas* needed some serious advice.

chapter two

Jake Murphy listened to the sexy voice on the answering machine for the dozenth time and felt the slow burn of pure lust settle low in his gut. That voice was a powerful weapon.

He popped the tape from the machine and put it in his desk drawer in case he was ever more desperate to hear the sound of a woman's voice than he was right now. No, not just any woman. *Her.* He'd never been so glad that George had decided to go visit his wife's family, even though there were more jobs to do than one man alone could handle.

It had been a long time since Jake had strapped on a tool belt. When he'd first started the business it had only been him and a few subcontractors hammering nails and putting up drywall. When the business had taken off because of its reputation for quality work, he'd made George a partner and Jake had donned a suit to meet with clients, lawyers and bankers. People liked to see a successful image before they handed you their money. But now with George on vacation he was back in the trenches and having the time of his life. The pleasure of watching something built from the ground up was still a part of him.

And Eve Lovegood had just risen to the top of the pile for purely selfish reasons. He was only a man after all. Surely George would understand the need to see if the face matched the voice. George would have done the same thing before he'd gotten himself shackled to a life sentence with one woman. Of course, George and Sally had been married for twenty-three years, so they were probably going to be okay.

Jake was simply curious as to the owner of the voice. It had been a while since he'd found a woman that intrigued him for more than just a quick roll in the hay. He was tired of the singles scene, but the word marriage still scared the hell out of him. Not everyone ended up in a bitter battle like his own parents had, fought and mapped out with the precision five star generals.

He shook his head to get rid of the memories and headed for the door, his brown leather jacket slung over his shoulder. The morning sun was still chasing the night away, and Jake ran his hand over the dark stubble he'd forgotten to shave that morning. He'd been so anxious to see whether or not that voice had been a product of his imagination that he'd only taken the time to jump into the shower and throw clothes on before heading to the office again.

What was he thinking? It was just a voice. She could be completely unattractive, married with three kids, or eighty and senile for all he knew. But if he kept her contained to his fantasies, she'd always be the seductive temptress he imagined her to be.

He'd been there the night before when she'd called, but had no intention of answering the phone that late, his desk already piled high with contracts needing his signature. And when her voice had come over the line he hadn't been in any shape to pick up the phone. That voice had given him a few incredible dreams during the night, and his curiosity couldn't be put on hold any longer. He only hoped she was an early riser because he wasn't going to wait a minute longer to make the face a reality.

The phone rang before he could get the door open and he felt his palms go sweaty at the thought that it might be *her* again. He made it back to his desk in two leaps and grabbed the receiver.

"It's about time you answered, boy. I could have died before you found your way to the phone. It's not nice to keep old people waiting. Our time is precious."

"You're going to live forever, Gran." Jake smiled into the phone at the voice of his favorite person, and he simply ignored her complaints of getting old.

Ruth Buchanan Murphy Stiles Littlefield Tyson O'Neil LaVelle was a woman to be reckoned with. She'd dropped all the other names after her last husband's death and gone back to using Murphy, because she said he was the one she loved best. She was ninety and acted like a teenager most of the time. She would outlive them all, and it looked like God was on her side.

"You're damned right, boy. I'm having too much fun. I'm thinking about getting a motorcycle. What do you think about that? We can cruise together. I want to get a hog just like yours."

Fear lodged somewhere in the pit of his stomach, not for her safety but for the safety of the other drivers on the road. Ruth Murphy hadn't had a driver's license since Reagan was president.

"Umm, I don't know. They're kind of big for someone your size, don't you think?"

"Yeah, you're probably right. That stupid man down at the DMV said I failed my test anyway. I've never failed at anything in my life. Murphy's do *not* fail."

"Except at marriage," Jake said.

"Not everyone's as stupid as your parents when it comes to love, boy. I loved every single one of my husbands, bless their souls. They don't make 'em like they used to though, so here I am alone again. That's why you should settle down now. You don't have too many good years left in you."

"I'm only thirty-two," Jake said, strangling on a laugh. The woman was outrageous.

"That doesn't mean a blasted thing. My third husband, Matthew Littlefield, was just your age when I married him, ten whole years younger than I was, and darned if he didn't croak at the most inopportune time. I had a hell of a time explaining to the police where I'd gotten the handcuffs from."

Jake looked at the small cabinet he kept behind his desk and wondered if it was too early for whiskey. It was barely seven thirty in the morning. There were some things grandchildren didn't need to know.

"Listen, Gran. I've got a job this morning." Memories of Eve Lovegood's voice sent tingles down his spine. He hadn't felt the anticipation of the mating dance in longer than he cared to remember. And if Eve Lovegood was even half as beautiful as she sounded then he was going to put his skills of seduction to the test. A voice that sexy had to come out of a mouth that could do incredible things.

"Well, let's get a move on, boy. I'm ready when you are. I was wondering how long you were going to stand there jawin' on the phone and leave me sitting in your driveway."

"You're sitting in my driveway right now?" Jake asked, all thoughts of the mystery woman's sexy voice completely lost because of one little old woman.

"You bet your boots I am. I had Edward drive me, the sweet man." Edward had been his grandmother's driver since before he was born. He'd always suspected there was something more than affection between them since she hadn't bothered to remarry after her last husband died thirty years ago. He'd never known his own grandfather, and barely remembered Ruth's sixth and final husband since he'd been scarcely more than a few years old when the man had died, but Edward had always been a constant in his life. One of the few.

"I've decided to stay for a while. I'll just go with you on the job, and Edward can take my bags to your house and get them settled in my room. Are you surprised, dear?"

Jake shouldn't have been surprised at all. Every

couple of years Ruth got a wild hair and decided to move in for a month or two before heading off somewhere else. The woman had wanderlust like he'd never seen before. Only now, her surprise trip seemed like a slight inconvenience with the thought of that voice playing in his mind. He stifled his thoughts with shame and decided to make the most of their visit. Just in case she didn't outlive everyone after all.

"That's great, Gran. We'll take my truck."

Jake hung up the phone and put his jacket on, his heart lighter and his conscience absolved. All of Gran's visits were memorable in his mind, and this one would be no different. He just had to watch her like a hawk, because she was a sneaky old lady and trouble followed her around every corner. He'd had to bail her out of jail on her last visit for chaining herself to a parking meter in front of the liquor store and protesting that they wouldn't sell her any booze on Sunday.

He locked the office behind him and wondered how he could have missed seeing the shiny black limo sitting in front of the Murphy-Madsen offices.

"You're as handsome as ever," Ruth said, giving him a surprisingly strong hug despite her thin bones.

"What can I say, I got all the Murphy good looks." Hair the color of good whiskey, eyes like the deepest part of the sea, and all the confidence of someone who knew exactly what his appeal was to the opposite sex.

"It's a cross to bear, I know, dear. Why do you think I've gone through so many husbands?"

He laughed and hoisted her into the cab of his Ford pickup, shiny red with the new smell barely clinging to the inside, and a silver toolbox attached to the bed.

"When did you get this hulk of machinery? Not that I'm complaining, mind you. Anything's an improvement over what you used to drive."

"The other one's in the car graveyard. couldn't do anything to save it."

"Thank God for that at least."

"Hey, it was a good truck."

"I'll never understand why you don't have every luxury at your fingertips with as much money as you have. I didn't work hard to leave it all to you and your cousin so you could live like a pauper."

"I'm just perverse that way, I guess."

"Just like your grandfather, bless his soul."

Jake decided not to ask. He didn't want to have any more unnecessary information about the people in his family tree. He turned onto Apple Tree Lane and looked for the house number Eve had left for him on the phone, but he was pretty sure which house was hers without looking at the mailbox number. It sat at the end of the cul-de-sac, a huge Victorian monstrosity that screamed horror movie.

"Holy God, would you look at that house?" Ruth said in awe.

Jake had a whole different feeling. Disaster. He hoped there was no one inside. By the looks of it, it could come down at any moment. But of course there was someone inside. There was a car parked in the driveway—a snappy little convertible that would be hell for him to get in and out of considering the length of his legs.

"I want you to stay here, Gran, until I know it's safe." *Which would be never.*

"It doesn't even look like the same house," she said in response.

Jake ignored her last comment, knowing she'd grown up in the area and had probably known the original owners. He made his way up the cracked sidewalk to the sagging front porch. He had his mini recorder ready and his notebook in hand, but he didn't think there was enough paper in the world for him to write down everything that was wrong with this house.

"Extensive structural damage to the frame of the house, the foundation's unlevel and seems to have sunk quite a bit on the north side. Rotten wood throughout, probably caused by termites. Structure was probably built in the late 1800s, sometime after the Civil War, indicated by the complication and mix of styles," he said into the recorder and then snapped it off.

This was part of his burden and his joy. He could see what the house had looked like in its youth. Three stories of Victorian elegance, angled bay windows and crumbling towers that flanked both sides, sweeping porches and weeping willows. Grand parties would be held often with couples in love sneaking kisses in a garden filled with climbing roses, the scent floating across the breeze on cool summer nights. He could fix it. He could fix anything. And then he'd offer to buy it from her for the full asking price. He wanted this house, termites and all.

He stepped gently up the stairs on the front porch, avoiding what looked like the weakest spots and praying that he left this meeting intact. He almost laughed out loud at the bright red welcome mat that sat in front of the door. Only if they had a death wish would anyone come to visit this woman.

There was an old fashioned doorbell, the kind you had to pull and usually sounded like a dying cat, but he didn't want the decibel level to start an avalanche, so he didn't touch it.

He took a deep breath and did what anyone else would have done. He knocked. And it turned out to be a mistake of epic proportions.

He watched in slow motion as the heavy door fell backwards to the floor, frame and all. And then he continued to watch, his mouth open but unable to get any sound out, as the door fell through to what looked like a basement below. He stood in the middle of a huge cloud of dust, his eyes closed, hoping he wasn't next when he heard the very voice he'd risked this death trap for.

"Oh, bother. Does everything have to fall through to the basement? I still haven't found the entrance yet."

Eve didn't notice the man standing in shock at her threshold. She was too busy cursing herself for thinking it would be fun to restore a house back to its former glory.

"Looks like you were right to call. I don't think I've ever met anyone in a more desperate situation," a husky voice said. The gruff timbre of it sent chills over her flesh, and she looked up in surprise.

The sight of the tall man in her doorway made her want to swallow her tongue. *Oh my.* This could not be George. George was supposed to be old, with wiry gray hair, milky blue eyes and overalls. This man was tall and muscled, with broad shoulders and narrow hips, dark brown hair with just a hint of red, and piercing blue eyes that made her forget she was supposed to be a professional. There would be a picture of this man under the definition of SEX in Webster's Dictionary. Not to mention he made denim look damn good.

"George?"

"No, I'm Jake Murphy. George is on vacation for a couple of weeks, so you get me instead."

The blush that tinged her cheeks was enough to tell him she'd picked up on the double meaning. It was her own fault. She shouldn't have looked at him like he was the flavor of the month at Ben and Jerry's.

"Oh, thank goodness. I thought my instincts had completely deserted me. You don't look anything at all what I expected a George to look like."

Jake took a minute to look over the voice he'd lusted after for less than twenty-four hours and found he was surprised as well. He'd expected a Kim Basinger look alike, somewhere along the line of Nine ½ Weeks. The kind of woman men fantasized about, but also the kind of woman that scared the hell out them in real life. Eve Lovegood couldn't have been more different, and he let out a quick sigh of relief.

The woman had dirt streaked across her nose and wore a man's dress shirt over tight jeans. Her black hair was pulled back with a scarf and her bright green eyes were giving him the once over. At first glance she looked like a delicate fairy princess, but she could never be mistaken for a fairy with eyes like that. She was a sorceress, with eyes brilliant and sharp enough to cut emeralds.

Boy, was he was toast. He rubbed his hand just under his heart and tried to catch his breath. He was about to say something that might get his face slapped when he heard the creak of the wood porch behind him. He whipped around and grabbed Ruth by the elbow before she ended up on the basement floor with the front door.

"Gran, I told you to stay in the truck. It isn't safe." He tried to turn her around and get her back down the stairs, but she dug in and stood her ground, all ninety-five pounds of her, and her gaze was glued to Eve Lovegood.

"Are you the owner of this house?" Ruth asked.

Eve had never been more embarrassed in her life. She knew money when she saw it, considering she'd grown up in the same world, and this woman had plenty of it. She looked down at her dusty clothes and dirty hands and fought the urge to hide them behind her back.

"Yes, ma'am. I'm Eve Lovegood."

"Good grief, girl. You bought the Shelley Sisters' Whorehouse. I haven't been here in ages."

chapter three

Jake tried to cover his laughter with a cough, but his Gran's spontaneity never left anyone bored. He looked over at Eve and hoped she wasn't too embarrassed by his grandmother's statement, because not everyone would be happy to know they'd bought a whorehouse. He was surprised to see excitement on her face.

"This is my grandmother, Ruth Murphy. You'll get used to her smart mouth after a while." He dodged her expected elbow and laughed at the mutinous expression on her face.

"You scamp. You've never been anything but trouble. Is that any way to talk about an old lady?"

"I don't see any old lady," he said giving her a wink.

The affection was obvious between the two, and

Eve was glad to know there was some substance beneath his looks because his grandmother looked like a handful. Ruth had a shocking sweep of white hair pulled back in a delicate coiffure and her high cheekbones spoke of breeding, but it was the sequined jeans and red leather jacket that had Eve raising an eyebrow. She was pretty sure she'd never met anyone as old as Ruth Murphy, and if she had she was pretty sure they all wore orthopedic shoes instead of red leather mules.

"It's nice to meet you. Was this really once a house of ill repute? How exciting." Eve stepped around some of the dark spots in the floor and grabbed on to Ruth's elbow. "I want to hear all about it. I knew this house had a sordid past. I could feel it as soon as I stepped through the door. Let's go into the kitchen and I'll fix you something to drink."

Jake stood cemented to the floor, unsure what had just happened to make him lose control of the situation. He followed them into the kitchen to find them a solid surface to sit on. He was a little surprised Eve could feel the sordid feelings in the house through the layers of dust and falling debris.

"Before you get started, ladies, let me make sure you're going to be okay in here. Eve, if you're planning on sleeping here we need to get started right away. My advice is to pack up and go to a hotel until we get the foundation leveled and the rotten wood torn out, but I can tell by looking at you that you're stubborn."

"I am not. I'm a perfectly reasonable human being, but I bought this house and I plan on sticking through to the end, no matter what happens."

"I figured as much. I'm going to do a walk through and make some notes so I can work up an estimate. If we can get everything nailed down today I can have a crew here first thing in the morning."

"I don't care about an estimate. I'll pay whatever it takes to get this place looking like it did when it was built."

"I'll pretend you didn't say that, since I'm a nice guy and don't want anyone to take advantage of you."

"You should listen to him, dear," Ruth said. "My Jake is one of the best men I've ever known. And he's single too. He's never even been engaged. I'm not saying he's not experienced. I don't want to give you that impression, but he's sowed his fair share of wild oats, so you don't have to worry about him fumbling around in the dark. What about you dear? Do you have a man in your life?"

Eve's face was as red as it could be under Ruth's not-so-subtle probing, but Jake wasn't about to throw her a life raft. He wanted to know the answer too.

"No, I'm not in a relationship." Not anymore, she added silently. "I'm pretty much married to my job."

The hands off signal couldn't have been any clearer to Jake, which made him want to get to know her even more. What were the secrets that Dr. Eve Lovegood kept hidden behind frosty indifference? He guessed he was more like his grandmother than he thought because this stubborn streak of his sure didn't come from his parents. They found very little in life that was worth breaking a sweat over. Not even their only son.

"What is it you do, dear? I know you have money and breeding. We can recognize our own, after all, but I take it you're involved in more than charities and endless functions?"

Eve thought that from anyone else the comment would have been unbearably snobby, but Ruth said it so matter-of-factly that Eve barely gave it a thought.

"I'm a therapist, but I don't have a private practice anymore. I have a show on the radio in the evenings, and I write weekly articles for the advice columns in the paper. I'll probably start seeing patients again after I get the house in order and an office set up."

"Dr. Lovegood?" Ruth asked, with awe. "I listen to your show every night. You give such good advice and you don't show any sympathy for those doormat women and pussy-whipped men that call in asking for a miracle."

Eve wasn't sure if she was more surprised that her sexy contractor's grandmother listened to her show or that she'd actually said the word pussy-whipped.

"A love doctor, huh?" Jake asked. He'd been still so long Eve had thought he'd already gone. "This should be interesting." He smiled, gave her a wink and walked away whistling, stepping around rotted boards and flipping his tape recorder on. "Just in case, make sure you listen for my screams of pain if there's some type of accident," he called out over his shoulder.

Oh, man. The guy had a set of dimples that wouldn't quit. She'd always been a sucker for dimples, but now she was in the same spot she always was. After a man found out she was supposed to know everything about relationships, they inevitably assumed she was some sort of sex goddess. She was tired of being a disappointment to men when they found she not only couldn't tell them the sexual secrets of the universe, but also that her only experiences with the act had left a great deal to be desired and a bitter taste in her mouth. Mediocre sex and even less affection was not a good foundation for marriage.

Maybe it was time to put on a brave front and pretend she was as worldly as she seemed. She turned back to Ruth. "So, tell me all about this whorehouse."

chapter four

Eve went over to her ice chest and wished she had something nicer to serve Ruth besides soft drinks and Ritz crackers.

"I have cola and water. What will it be?" Eve asked rummaging around in her backpack to see if there were any more Oreos.

"I'll have a cola. It'll drive Jake crazy," Ruth said with a bit of devilment. Eve had a feeling that Jake got his trouble making abilities honestly.

"I don't want you to get in trouble." She arranged the cookies on a paper plate and got two cans of cola out of the ice chest. She didn't even have cups to pour them in.

"I won't get in trouble. Jake's a big softy at heart. And even if he wasn't, I wouldn't care. I'm old enough to get to do what I want to. I could die at any moment, you know."

"I doubt that," Eve said. "You seem pretty spry to me."

"I am that. I've buried six husbands, and not one of them could ever keep up with me. It's a damn shame that men are such fragile creatures."

Eve sat down at the card table and chuckled. "I wonder why the realtor didn't tell me this place had a history."

"He probably didn't want to add any more black marks against its character. It's not exactly in top form."

"Yeah, but I would have bought it sooner had I known."

Ruth smiled and laid her hand lightly on Eve's arm. "More girls should be like you," she said. "You remind me a bit of myself, though a little more uptight. We'll work on that and see if I can be a bad influence."

Eve's mouth hung open at the uptight remark, but Ruth didn't seem at all contrite that she might have insulted her.

"Margaret and Myrtle Shelley opened a high class bordello right after the First World War ended in 1918. They'd both lost their husbands overseas, and I guess they figured their prospects for another marriage weren't all that great, so they opened this place up and just called it Shelley's. And they did a right fine business, too."

Ruth's eyes softened as she remembered. They were good memories, memories that held joy and youth.

"Now when prohibition came along in the Twenties you can imagine that it put a severe dent in their business, so they turned the basement into a private bar and the place became a speakeasy. I was barely seventeen the first time I stepped foot into this place, newly married to Jake's grandfather and green as an ear of corn. The Shelley sisters were quite a bit older by the time I made my appearance here, but they were still going strong."

A wistful smile tilted the corners of her mouth as she wetted her throat with the forbidden cola, and Eve felt like she was intruding on something special and private.

"What a handsome man my Mitch was, and such a gentleman. I felt like a princess in a fairytale the first time I laid eyes on him. He was an experienced lover, which is something I'll always be grateful for, but after he took those vows he was devoted to me until the day he died. I lost him in the war, you know."

Eve blinked the tears from her eyes. She couldn't imagine experiencing so many things in so short a time. Loss was never easy, no matter what the circumstances.

"Don't be sad dear. We had ten glorious years together and made two children between us. I see him every time I look at Jake, so it makes the memories a little sweeter. But, oh the adventures we had together, and I'm glad to say I've had quite a few more over the years."

Eve was in awe. What an amazing woman, barely a girl out of the schoolroom and so unafraid of the life that lay ahead of her. She was envious of Ruth's courage, and wished that she hadn't been so sheltered for the last thirty years.

"You understand, as someone of my social position, I would have been in a heap of trouble had my parents found out. They would have disowned me in a heartbeat if I'd brought scandal to the family name. But my husband took care of the details, and I learned to gamble, drink whiskey and keep my husband entertained in the bedroom so he never had reason to visit the rooms above the first floor."

"Wow," Eve said, impressed. "Your secrets are safe with me."

"Well, it hardly matters anymore since my parents have been dead near forty years now and all my other friends keep dying too. It's damned inconvenient to get old, let me tell you."

Jake watched the two women from the doorway. He'd loved his grandmother all his life. She'd been the calm in the storm through a tumultuous childhood. And he was beginning to believe that he'd loved Eve Lovegood since the moment he'd heard her voice on his answering machine. Who would have though that Jake Murphy would take the fall because of a tiny sorceress with a smoky voice and a kind heart?

"Are you about ready to go, Gran?" Both women looked up at him with identical expressions of annoyance, and he had to bite the inside of his cheek to keep from laughing. He turned his attention to Eve. "The foundation isn't in as bad a shape as I thought it was. It just needs to been shored up and leveled, but it isn't cracked. The safest way for us to start things is by filling in the basement, so you'll have a solid surface. I'll get a team started on it first thing in the morning."

Eve nodded, hoping he knew what he was doing.

"I've moved your things to the safest place I could find so you don't have to worry about toilets falling on your head."

"Oh, thanks," Eve said, flustered by the way he was looking at her, as if he knew a secret and wasn't quite ready to let her in on it yet. For someone who was supposed to be good with words she felt decidedly lacking in that department at the moment.

"What time do you go into the station tonight?"

"I go in for a quick briefing at five and then I go on air from six to nine. I'm usually home by ten."

"I'm going to come back later this evening and start work on the rotted wood. That will give me time to go back to the office, work everything up on paper and call in enough crews to get started."

He didn't bother to mention that he was going to have some unhappy foremen pulling up stakes in the middle of other jobs to start a new project, but he'd make the pay worth their while, so they wouldn't complain for too long. "The water and electricity will probably be able to be turned on sometime next week."

"That would be great. Mrs. Larsen next door has been letting me use her downstairs bathroom so I can get ready for work, and I've just been eating takeout until I have a workable room."

He'd wondered where she'd been showering and was ready to beg for her to use his place if she needed one. He was going to be seeing a lot of Eve Lovegood. He'd make sure of it.

"*Frustrated in Fairfield*, you're on the air with Dr. Lovegood. What can I do for you tonight?" Eve cringed at the high pitch squeal that came through her headphones. "You'll have to turn the radio down, sir."

She waited patiently for the mumbling and squealing to wind down. After all, it was a full moon Friday and she'd been having weird conversations all night. But what she'd never been while working was distracted. A pair of cobalt blue eyes and twin dimples kept invading her concentration to the point where she'd had to ask a caller to repeat his problem twice.

"Yeah, um, Dr. Lovegood? This is. . ."

"We don't say names on the air, sir," she reminded the caller as the sensor bleeped out his name. For some reason people always wanted to give their names before telling her embarrassing things about their personal life. She'd never understand it.

"Yeah, um, anyway. I'm having a problem with my girlfriend. Or I guess she's my ex-girlfriend now. She keeps calling and bothering me, leaving messages on my machine, and that makes my new girlfriend really mad. What should I do to get my ex to leave me alone?"

"How long ago did you break up with your girlfriend?"

"What's today? Friday?"

"Yes," Eve said, already impatient with the caller.

"Then it was Wednesday."

"And when did you acquire your new girlfriend." Anybody that knew Eve well knew the particular tone of voice she was using said you might want to take cover, but *Frustrated in Fairfield* wasn't too bright.

"Oh, my new girlfriend and I have been together a couple of weeks. Is that important?"

Eve stifled a scream and wondered how this idiot could have passed the screening process to be on the air, and then she remembered he was one of the better callers she'd had all night.

"Maybe your ex-girlfriend doesn't feel like she's attained closure. The breakup seems to have happened rather abruptly. How did you break up with her?"

"I sent her a text message, and she was lucky she got that. Those things are expensive. Lola, that's my new girlfriend, thinks we need to save every penny so we can get married, but with Justine calling and leaving all those messages on the machine it's making things a little difficult between Lola and me. What should I do?"

"So you cheated on your first girlfriend and then had the audacity to break up with her by text message? And now when she's calling to find out what's going on, you don't have the guts to pick up the phone and tell her? Have I got the facts straight?"

"Yeah, I guess so, but you make it sound kinda harsh."

Eve didn't care. There had to be justice out there for the people who got screwed by love. "What did you say your name was?" she asked.

"Jeremy Kline. But, hey, I thought we weren't supposed to give our names."

"I've decided to make an exception in your case. My advice to you, Jeremy, is to grow a spine and a decent amount of morals before you try your hand at relationships again. My advice to the women of Fairfield is to run far in the opposite direction if you see Jeremy Kline coming your way. He has a lot to learn."

Eve cut the connection and gave the notice for a commercial break before falling back in her chair with a disgusted sigh.

"Whoa, what was that all about?" Lucy asked, sticking her head in the door.

"I don't know. I just snapped. I want to talk to a normal person."

"Well, the phone lines have started lighting up like crazy, so a bunch of normal people are calling in to support you or you've just given the green light for all the crazies to crawl out of the woodwork."

"Wonderful." Eve took a drink of water and put

her headset back on. It was eight-forty-five. She could last another fifteen minutes. And then she was going to set the record for leaving the building and getting home on the off chance that Jake Murphy was still inside her house.

Maybe a quick fling was just the thing she needed. Millions of people did it. Not everything had to end in marriage. Lord knew there was a slim chance she'd ever go that route again. The problem was, she was one of the few people in the world who related sex and marriage as two sides of the same coin. She didn't tell her listeners that because who'd want to listen to her then? But she'd been a virgin when she'd married and she hadn't been with anyone since. Hadn't wanted to be, she clarified.

She looked at the information from her next caller and hoped for normalcy.

"*Waiting in Dallas*, this is Dr. Lovegood, what can I do for you tonight?"

"Hey, Doc."

Eve froze at the sound of the familiar voice on the other end of the line and felt her insides do a slow flip. Maybe she was thinking about him so hard he'd picked up on the signals.

"Hey, yourself," she said, her voice more husky than usual.

"I was hoping you could help me out with something."

"What's that?"

"Well, there's this woman."

Eve felt a quick stab of jealousy clutch her heart because of this nameless woman. She ruthlessly stomped it back down and took a deep breath. She was a professional.

"What woman?" The question didn't really come out as professional as she'd hoped, more of a snarl.

Jake laughed, sending shivers straight down to her toes. "Do you believe in love at first sight, Doc?"

"Well, I suppose so, but more often than not it's usually lust at first sight. Is that what you have?"

"No, it's definitely love. You see, a woman left a message on my business answering machine yesterday, and the sound of her voice made me throw all my well laid plans out the window. I had to meet her, so I went to her house this morning to see how I could be of service. One look at those amazing green eyes and I was head over heels, just like that."

"You seem to be pretty sure of your feelings. Are you a man who falls in and out of love easily?"

"No. Can't ever say I've felt anything close to it other than what I have for my family. The truth is, I've tried to avoid it. I've enjoyed the bachelor's life over the years, but I was hit square between the eyes today. What do you think I should do?"

"Well, if it were me, I'd want to get to know this woman a little better than just the superficial impressions you got from one meeting. She could be a serial killer or organize her pantry in alphabetical order by can size. And if I were this woman, I don't think I'd fall for the love at first sight bit, especially if you've been enjoying the bachelor life the way I think you have, so you might want to keep that to yourself. Romancing the right woman is hard work. And you might be surprised. She might not want to settle down in a relationship. Maybe she has plans or dreams she wants to act on. Or maybe she has a difficult time with relationships. She could even be a lesbian for all you know."

"Do you think she'd tell me all these things if I asked her out on a date?"

"I think it's a good place to start."

"What if she turns me down?"

"You sound like a pretty nice guy. I would think she'd at least give you a chance."

"I hope so, the problem is, whenever I'm around her all I can think about is taking her into my arms and getting lost in her eyes. They bewitch me."

Eve caught her sigh before it could go out over the airwaves.

"Thanks for all your help, Doc. It sounds like she needs to be swept off her feet, and I think I'm exactly the guy to do that."

Eve somehow got her voice and her hormones under control enough to thank the caller and sign off, but it was all a blur. Jake had used up every bit of her last fifteen minutes, and she would give him anything he wanted just from saving her from any more lunatics.

"Whew," Lucy said as she burst in the room, a bundle of energy spiked with coffee. "That guy was hot."

"You don't even know what he looks like. How can you tell he's hot? I thought you didn't like men?"

"I don't have to see that man to know he's hot. He just made every woman in America wish she was the woman he fell in love with. How romantic. Even I could be turned with someone like that. And I could tell you weren't all that unaffected either."

Eve knew her face was flushed so she bent over to grab her bag to give her heart rate a little time to slow.

"I'm going to go ahead and take off. There are going to be construction workers swarming my house at the crack of dawn tomorrow."

"Oh, good. Everything worked out with the number you called."

"It worked out magnificently," Eve said with a

secret smile. "I'll never be able to thank you enough for giving me that card. I have a good feeling about Murphy-Madsen construction."

Lucy watched her friend head off to the elevators, her step more lively than usual, and wondered what the hell she'd just missed.

chapter five

The brittle October morning rang crisp and clear as the sunlight peaked over the horizon. Eve was freezing and stood impatiently over the camping stove she had sitting on the floor as she waited for the water to boil for her coffee.

The sun was still tucked away in sleep when she'd woken to start her day. She showered, thanks to Mrs. Larsen's generosity, and dressed warmly in jeans and a turtleneck and then threw a flannel shirt on top of it all. Goosebumps still lined her flesh, but she planned to warm up soon enough. If only the damned coffee would make. This was her house, and she had every intention of helping with the renovations. Her hands could get dirty just as well as anyone else's. A little hard work would warm her up almost as fast as coffee.

Workers began arriving at a steady pace at six o'clock, but the one person she was looking for was nowhere to be found. Maybe he'd changed his mind and decided to run far, far away, clinging to his bachelorhood like a second skin.

"Come on, come on," she said as she stamped her feet, wishing the saying weren't true about a watched pot never boiling.

"You look pretty desperate for caffeine."

Eve jerked around to face the door and felt the air close off from her lungs. He hadn't run away after all. And he'd brought coffee.

"Is that for me?" she asked, pointing to the cup that flashed the name of her favorite coffee establishment.

"Yeah, I meant to use it as a bribe, but you kind of have a crazy look in your eyes so I think I might just set it down slowly and run for the door. I've seen that same look in my Gran's eyes before, and it usually ends with me having to bail her out of jail."

"Hand it over, and I'll do whatever it is you'd planned to bribe me with. I'm desperate."

"I have to ask you something important first."

"What?"

"Are you an obsessive compulsive pantry organizer, and if not, do you have an aversion to settling down in a serious relationship?"

"Oh, man, I really need that coffee."

Jake moved forward slowly, the coffee held out as a peace offering, and started laughing when she jerked it out of his grasp and took a scalding sip. He put his own cup down and backed her against the kitchen counter.

"That's a dangerous power you just gave me. If I wasn't such an honorable guy, I could think of all sorts of things for you to do to pay me back for a simple cup of coffee."

"You don't seem like the kind of man who knows the meaning of the word simple."

He switched their positions so he was leaning against the counter and she was embraced in the circle of his arms, and the look on her face was somewhere between curious and scared to death. Dr. Lovegood was an interesting combination, and he should have believed her when she'd told him that really romancing a woman would take a lot of hard work.

"I'm going to go out on a limb, since you didn't bother to answer my questions, and say that you aren't completely crazy. But by the wary look in your eyes I might have to do a lot of fast talking to make you consider a relationship."

Eve couldn't seem to get a deep breath into her lungs, and little spots danced in front of her eyes. Her coffee had ended up somewhere, forgotten as soon he'd taken her in his arms. She might not have a lot of experience, but she knew when a man was going to kiss her. His eyes were endless pools of blue, so dark with desire and longing that she took an automatic step back.

His hands stopped her retreat and gently rubbed the tightened muscles in her back. She shivered at his touch, and felt the throb of attraction low in her body. Moisture pooled between her thighs, and she lowered her head in embarrassment at her instant arousal to his touch. She'd never felt like this with anyone.

The heat of his fingers branded her with every touch against her spine. He tipped her chin up with his finger and leaned in close so their breaths mingled. She didn't know how to describe the ferocity of need that claimed her body, but she knew it terrified her to the depths of her soul— terrified her enough to make him stop before things got out of hand.

"Don't kiss me," she gasped.

"Why not? Did you forget to brush your teeth? I don't mind, honestly."

"No, they're brushed."

"Well, then, there's no problem," he said, moving in again.

Eve pushed her hands against his chest so he bumped against the counter, and the cabinet door that had been hanging precariously at best fell off and hit Jake on the head.

"Ouch, son of a bitch." He rubbed the top of his head furiously and gave her a glare as if to place the blame on her shoulders.

"Let me see," Eve said pushing him into a nearby folding chair. "Is it bleeding?"

"You did that on purpose."

Eve barely contained a laugh at the disgruntled expression on Jake's face, more suited to a ten year old boy than a grown man.

"I did not. Stop being such a baby and let me see." She ran her hands along his scalp and felt the gentle swelling of the lump that had already formed. "There, it's not so bad. Just a bump. Take two Aspirin and call me in the morning." She leaned over and kissed it before she could talk herself out of it.

Jake grabbed hold of her hand and swung her around so she sat in his lap.

"Let me up. I don't want your workers to think improper things about me."

"They wouldn't dare. I'd fire every one of them first."

"Exactly, and then my house wouldn't get fixed."

"Why is kissing a bad idea? The truth this time."

"What if we weren't very good at it?"

Jake laughed uproariously, his body shaking so hard he nearly dislodged Eve onto the floor.

"It wasn't that funny," Eve said, slightly miffed.

"Are you kidding me? There are some things you just know by instinct. You're right. It wouldn't be good."

Eve felt a sliver of disappointment that he hadn't pressed the issue a little longer.

"It would be amazing," he said softly. He leaned in close so the words whispered directly into her ear, and he nipped the lobe slightly, eliciting a moan from deep inside her. "There wouldn't be words to describe it. I thought about it last night when I called into your show, and every time your breath hitched over the air, I thought about how out of all the people who were listening, your sighs were only for me. And then I thought about staying here, so I could take advantage of those sighs when you walked in the door, but I made myself go home and spent a sleepless night thinking about you. But you're right. It's much too soon for kissing. I can see I'm going to have to re-strategize."

"I'm just not very good at this sort of thing," Eve confessed, lowering her gaze to the buttons on his shirt. His body heat was astounding. She didn't think she'd ever be cold again.

"But you're the Love Doctor." The way she went rigid in his arms was enough to tell him it had been the wrong thing to say. He could have kicked himself for being so stupid.

"Exactly. I give people advice on their love lives. That doesn't mean I want one of my own. Men seem to be either terrified of me or they think I'm some kind of sex goddess. You're not in love with me, and I don't want to start something that has the potential to leave me in pieces."

"I see," Jake said. And he did see. "It sounds as if you're talking from experience. I don't think I like being compared to another man."

"Let me go."

The frigid silence he was met with was enough to tell him that he'd struck a chord. Eve needed a full fledged romance, so she wouldn't even realize until it was too late that he'd wedged himself into her heart. And then he'd get her to tell him what secrets were weighing so heavily in her mind.

"No, I don't think I will let you go, but I'll hold off on the kissing. For now," he added. "How about I bring you coffee every morning and fresh donuts?"

"I don't like donuts." She tried to relax and take the olive branch he'd extended. "But I adore chocolate Éclairs," she said with a calculating look and a raised eyebrow that made him laugh.

"Okay, fresh coffee and chocolate Éclairs. And then I'll bring you dinner every night until I get your kitchen finished and you can cook for me."

"First of all," she said, holding up a finger, "I work in the evenings. I usually pick something up on the way to the station. Second, I've never cooked a day in my life. A woman named Gretchen has fed me since I was just a little girl and she'll continue to do so when my kitchen's finished. She refuses to move in to the carriage house until the house is fixed."

"Smart woman. Do you think Gretchen would cook for me too?"

"No. Hire your own cook. Your grandmother tells me you have plenty of money that you just leave lying around so you can pretend to be common like most of the rest of the world."

"I've decided to put my inheritance in a trust fund for our children. It's never too early to plan for the future. All right, never mind," he said before she could utter a protest. "Don't get overexcited. You're kind of high strung, but I think I like that in a woman."

"How dare you…"

"Shh," he said pressing his finger to her lips. "I wouldn't want you to say something you'll regret later. Here's my final offer. We'll have lunch together here during the weekdays, where I'll quietly romance you and make you fall madly in love with me. I'll take you out someplace nice on the weekend then seduce you. Or maybe we could skip some of the middle parts and go right to the seduction. I have an awful need to taste you."

"Umm…I think maybe we should keep our mind on food for the time being."

"You'll never look at food the same once you've had a meal with me. I wonder what champagne would taste like if I drank it from you skin." He skimmed his finger from just behind her ear to her full bottom lip.

"You could make me want you," Eve said, unsteadily. "And I might give in to the temptation. But I'm not going to change my mind on things getting serious between the two of us. I can't do it. I *won't* do it."

"I know exactly what I'm getting into. I love you, Eve, whether you believe me or not. It only took a second, and I'm not afraid to work hard to get you to love me back. Now let's get you out of here. The kitchen's one of the first things on the agenda."

He stood and slapped her on the butt like he'd just hit a line drive down the middle, before grabbing her hand and pulling her out the door.

Eve wasn't sure what had just happened, other than the fact that Jake thought he loved her and was going to wait patiently until she could get her act together. He didn't seem like the type who was used to rejection.

"What's that?" Eve asked, looking at the large trailer that was hooked up to the back of Jake's pick up.

"That's my traveling office, so I can deal with paperwork while I'm on site. It's fully stocked with a kitchenette, a bathroom and a bed, so you shouldn't be too uncomfortable while we're working. I'm going to leave it here so you can get a decent night's sleep and not worry about things crashing down on your sleeping body."

Eve pulled out of his grasp. "But I wanted to help with the house," she said, her arguments already forming on her lips.

"You can help when it's time to make decisions on structural changes or color schemes. But I need your help with something else while I'm working. You see, if Gran isn't kept occupied, she has a tendency to get into trouble. You'd be doing me a big favor if you spent a little time with her in the day. You can even bring your work in here with you and set up your own office space."

Eve already knew she was beaten. If he didn't want her under foot all he had to do was say so. He didn't have to stick her with babysitting duty just to keep her distracted. Sneaky man.

"Fine," she said primly. "I'd love to spend the days with your grandmother. I'm sure I'll get quite the education. Maybe she'll loosen me up a little. You were the one who called me high strung a few minutes ago, weren't you?" Eve batted her eyelashes at Jack and hid her grin at his scowl.

"Now wait a minute…"

"No, no, Jake. You go ahead and do all your manly building things, and your grandmother and I will keep ourselves occupied."

Jake wasn't sure he liked the look in Eve's eyes. He got a sudden image of Eve and his grandmother behind bars, cheating the other prisoners out of cigarettes, and a cold sweat broke out on his body. His grandmother could lead a saint down the path to temptation. He was about to call off the whole thing when the bad influence in question came into sight.

"It's about time you two got here," Ruth said. "It's not safe to leave an old lady alone for very long. What if I had a stroke or slipped in the shower? Didn't I tell you that you wouldn't be able to talk her into anything on the spur of the moment? Eve's not like those other bird-brained floozies you've dated in the past. She's not going to just fall into your arms when you twinkle those baby blues her way."

Eve blushed crimson, embarrassed because she'd done just that. And liked it too. But she definitely had questions about the bird-brained floozies. She might be naïve when it came to love, but she knew very well what jealousy felt like. Her marriage had been full of it, and if Jake Murphy had that in common with her husband, he might as well give up now.

Jake was going to have to work really hard to prove that what he felt was more than a simple case of infatuation. She knew herself well enough to know that once her heart was given to a man, it would be his forever.

chapter six

Two days later, Eve pulled her silver Miata in front of her house and blew out a breath.

"Things have to get worse before they can get better," she told herself, looking at the debris and materials that sat in semi-organized piles around her lawn.

She was grateful to Jake for letting her stay in the trailer while the construction was going on. She couldn't have lived in that rubble, stubborn independence set aside.

Eve stepped out of the car and tried to subdue her hair. It was just past noon and already it looked as if it had been through World War III. She'd had an early meeting with her editor at the paper, and damned if she wasn't tired of having people try to manipulate her time for their own selfishness.

They wanted her to branch out to a daily column instead of her usual once a week editorial that appeared in the big Sunday paper. She'd said no. And it came down to her own selfish reasons. She just didn't want to do it. Plain and simple. Her schedule was already more than full with the radio show and the occasional guest appearances she made at universities and television networks. She was scheduled to teach a class on love and marriage next semester at the local college, not to mention the new headache of her house.

And then there was the note. It had been folded neatly under her windshield wiper, and if it hadn't had had her name printed on the outside she would have thrown it away without reading it. She wished she had. She got the occasional nutcase that followed her show from time to time. She'd get personal calls at home wanting advice or someone who fancied themselves in love with her voice. But the note had taken her off guard.

The man, at least she assumed it was a man, had only written that he'd been watching her and that she was as beautiful in real life as she was on the radio. There was no signature. So she'd shoved it to the bottom of her purse and watched her rearview mirror all the way home. Her nerves were strung taught between her editor and her admirer and all she wanted was a very large glass of wine for lunch and a double fudge sundae for dessert.

She was dressed in a black suit, a pencil skirt that came just above the knee and a jacket that covered a cream colored shell, complete with the dreaded pantyhose. That was another reason she hated going into the city to meet with her editor. The man always insisted they meet for breakfast or lunch at some pricey restaurant. Someday, she was going to demand he meet on her ground, and she was going to require him to wear sweatpants and a ratty t-shirt just to be contrary.

"Stupid man. Pantyhose Nazi. Demanding that I drop everything and dress up so he can look down my blouse and tell me he wants a column seven days a week." Men weren't exactly on her list of most favorite things at the moment.

Jake noticed the minute Eve pulled up in front of the house. He considered himself a pretty good judge of women and knew enough to recognize when one was working up a serious mad.

She looked like a wild woman, her hair at crazy angles and muttering to herself under her breath. His workers were giving her a wide berth, and one even went so far as to cross himself when he passed by. But boy did that skirt do something spectacular to her legs. She was curvy and soft in all the right places, and he was finding being patient wasn't nearly as easy as he thought it would be.

He'd worked on the kitchen for the last two weeks, tearing out and rebuilding, staying out of the plumber's way and keeping an extra eye on his grandmother. The sight of Eve was exactly what his tired eyes needed. His grandmother was gone for the afternoon, getting her nails done and her skin buffed, or some such nonsense, but she managed to look twenty years younger so he guessed it was worth it. Eve was all his for the time being.

The sound of a shrill scream brought him out of his daydream and running out the door. Eve was plastered to the sidewalk with her hands over her head and little whimpers escaping from somewhere under the pile of hair.

"What happened? What's wrong? Are you hurt?" Jake ran his hands over her back and legs, looking for an injury since her words weren't coherent enough for him to understand.

She pointed up to the sky and it was then he noticed the bats that were swooping from the trees. Their home must have been disturbed by whoever was working on the top floor.

"Relax, Eve. It's just a few bats. There are workers on the top floor that must have disturbed their nest. They won't hurt you."

Eve had had enough of dealing with men for the day, and her temper got the better of her. "How do you know they won't hurt me? You never mentioned that you were a bat expert as well as a womanizer. How ever have you managed to fit everything into such a tight schedule?""Uhh. . .I think this is one of those moments where a man's best defense is to say nothing. But you might want to tone the yelling down a bit. Your neighbors are starting to enjoy the show."

"Coward," she said, scrambling up off the ground. "And I never yell, so they can all just find something else to stare at."

Eve turned and faced down the first neighbor she saw. "You there," she said pointing to a man standing on his lawn and watering his flowers. "What's your name?"

"Mr. Panamaker," he stammered.

"Well, I hope in the future you won't make a habit of eavesdropping on private conversations. I didn't say a word when your wife locked you out of the house in your underwear last week."

"No, ma'am," he said, looking like a frightened rabbit that wanted nothing more than to hide under the bushes.

"Well, then," Eve said, satisfied. "I'm planning on having a neighborhood barbeque when the house is finished. I hope you and your wife will come."

"Yes, ma'am," he said, putting down the hose and inching his way towards his front door slowly.

Jake wasn't sure if laughing was the right thing to do under the circumstances, so he disguised it with a cough and hid his smile behind his hand.

"Sometimes, you remind me of my granny," he said. "Very scary."

She looked down at her leg and noticed the blood seeping from her knee. On the bright side, there was a good sized rip in her hated pantyhose. "Same damned knee I hurt when I fell through the back porch."

"Uh, huh. I didn't realize you were the one who'd done all that damage. You were lucky you didn't break your neck. Let's go get you cleaned up, crazy lady," he said, pushing her in the direction of the trailer.

"I'm perfectly capable of taking care of myself."

He ignored her protests and picked her up in his arms. "I know you are, but I'd prefer to do it myself. I'd never want you to say that I hadn't acted like a gentleman."

Eve felt lower than dirt. There was no reason for her to take out her bad mood on Jake. He hadn't done anything wrong. Well, maybe she did have a little bit of resentment over the outcome of their first date. It wasn't his fault that an old girlfriend had showed up at the restaurant where they were having dinner. And he couldn't have known that another of his ex's would show up at the club he'd taken her to for dancing. It was all just a big coincidence. But she had to wonder if he'd told those women how much he loved them before he got them into bed. Was it the thrill of the chase that had him so enamored with her? The similarities to Steve were piling up, and the smart thing to do would be to get as far away from Jake as possible.

"I'm sorry for being such a bitch."

"No, problem," he said, reaching for the first aid kit as soon as they made it inside of the trailer. "Everyone's entitled every now and then. You want to tell me about it?"

"I just had a lousy meeting with the editor of the paper I write for. I don't know, maybe I'll stop writing for the paper all together. I've been toying with the idea of putting a book together and I've had a call from a publisher that's interested in the finished product. I have hundreds of letters that never get answered in the paper. I could use some of them in the book and give a few extra tips or ideas that don't ever get printed."

"Sounds to me like you've given it more than a little thought. Take your pantyhose off so I can doctor that scrape."

Eve eyed him wearily, wondering if this was just

the excuse he needed to get his hands on her. Her knee was throbbing, though, so she did as he asked.

"I don't think this is going to work, Jake."

"I haven't even put the medicine on it yet. I'm a very competent medic."

"That's not what I meant, and you know it. I don't think you and I are going to work. I've had some time to think about this over the last couple of days, and I don't think I'm ready for a relationship just yet. I've got a lot of baggage and resentment that I'm obviously still carrying around."

What she really meant was that she couldn't take it if Jake Murphy broke her heart and went on to another in his long line of conquests. How would she feel if she ran into him in a restaurant with his new girlfriend? The answer to that was simple— she'd have to kill the woman.

"Are you ever going to tell me about this man who broke your heart and left me with such a difficult job? I bet I could help you get over him."

"Doubtful. You seem to share some of his qualities."

"Hmm," was the only response that declaration got out of him. She was almost positive he'd have more to say than a measly hmm.

"Is that all you're going to say?" She demanded, knowing she'd just jumped overboard to the role of totally irrational female.

"No. I'm going to concentrate on your knee and pretend that you just told me how much you love being with me. If you can live in a fantasy world, there's nothing to say that I can't join you there. Did I tell you my partner, George, is coming back from vacation tomorrow?" He didn't wait for her answer. "I'll be glad to have him back. I've put off several meetings because I've had to wear my hard hat instead of a suit. Don't worry though. I'll still pay special attention to your house. You could say it's become a pet project of mine."

Eve didn't respond, but fell victim to the caress of his voice as he put something cold on the scrapes at her knee.

Jake was tired of being patient, and it was a strain to not let his irritation show at being labeled lecher for life. Did she not believe in change or redemption for past mistakes? For someone as smart as she was, she couldn't see past the end of her nose when it came to her own love life. Before either one of them could say anything they were likely to regret, he leaned down and kissed her knee gently. Her indrawn breath was enough to tell him that she was already in way over her head. He just had to do everything in his power to make her realize it.

"I've got to get back to work," he said. "Some

eccentric doctor bought this dilapidated house of ill repute and wants a miracle. I figure I'd better give her what she wants since her sanity seems to be a bit fragile."

Jake left her sitting in his trailer, a look of utter surprise and something else on her face. He wanted to believe it was longing. Things were falling into place nicely.

chapter seven

"You've already had callers on hold for more than an hour tonight, and you haven't even gone on the air yet," Lucy said, her ever present clipboard in her hands and five pencils stuck every which way in her hair.

"I've pulled two interns to help me screen the calls. You have a couple of repeats we'll put through so you can hear their progress. Oh, and don't drink the coffee. Miles Webber drank two cups and had to be rushed to the hospital with chronic nausea. I swear the man lost twenty pounds in ten minutes. I'm thinking about taking some home with me in case I want to start a new diet."

Eve let her friend's words wash over her, used to the woman's constant rambling, and looked over her notes for the show. She *would* pick tonight to talk about the key ingredients to a successful relationship.

She chose her topics for every show weeks in advance so advertising would know how to market, and also so she could do a few promos for the upcoming week. She would pay any amount of money for someone to tear her notes to shreds and let her talk about something more mundane—like the importance of couples therapy or masturbation techniques.

"Well, let's get started," Eve said, already thinking of Jake, not that he'd ever really left her thoughts.

She'd snuck out of the house when she'd left for the station, not sure she could be so close to him again without going up in flames. The heart was a damned nuisance, and when her logical brain got involved it became an even bigger one.

"Hey, are you all right?" Lucy asked, concerned. "You seem a little down."

"I'm fine. Just a little tired"

"I've never seen you tired. You're the Energizer Bunny. There's something else going on and don't think I won't figure it out. I've got the nose of a bloodhound."

"Maybe I should say I'm not ready to talk about it instead."

"That, I'll accept. But I'll ask again," Lucy said,

leaving the booth for her own desk on the other side of the glass enclosure.

"I'd expect nothing less," Eve muttered, adjusting her headset and listening to the fade out of the upbeat music that always introduced her show. She took her cue from Lucy and wiped her sweaty palms on her blue jeans.

"Welcome to the show. This is Dr. Eve Lovegood, and tonight's topic is something that affects every single one of us whether we want it to or not. No matter what stance we take on the subject, no matter what our race or sexual orientation—it affects us all. *Relationships.* What is the key ingredient to keep your relationship from falling apart? Is it one specific thing? Is love enough, or are there several ingredients that must be measured and combined before you have a healthy, lasting, loving relationship? And most importantly, where does trust fit into the mix? We'll talk about the answers to those questions tonight, and I welcome you to call in and share your own experiences or ask questions."

Eve settled into the comfort of familiarity. She'd never minded giving lectures, but there was something missing tonight. She read the words from the page, her voice compelling and clear, but her heart wasn't in it. She was too busy keeping her mind and heart blocked off from listening to her own advice.

"*Infatuated in San Francisco*, you're on the air."

"Um, yeah. I have a question about women."

"Okay. What about women?" Eve had no idea where her patience had gone, but for some reason it had deserted her tonight.

"Well, it's just they're so confusing. How am I supposed to know what my fiancée wants when she says one thing but means another? And then she gets mad because I don't know what's wrong. What should I do?"

"It sounds to me like the two of you have some communication issues to work out. Do you always tell your fiancée what you're feeling?"

"No, but that's different. Guys aren't supposed to do stuff like that."

"Maybe you're both building your relationship on misconceptions, and it won't be long before it crumbles to the ground. Your fiancée obviously believes you should know her well enough to read her mind, and you feel because you're a man, it gives you the right to keep things bottled up inside. I want you to both make a list of everything that bothers you about each other, no matter how small, and then I want you to make another list of the things you love about each other. Read over each other's lists and then talk about how the list makes you feel. These are things that need to be said before you say I do. Otherwise, several years and a couple of kids later, the things will come back to blow up in your face."

Eve looked at the flashing lights on her control panel and then at the clock. She was going to go insane sitting here for the next two hours. Why hadn't she had the courage to tell Jake that she was afraid? Afraid of losing her heart to someone who was bound to break it? She couldn't go through the pain of betrayal again, of being a noose around any man's neck, as Steve had so often liked to remind her. She'd had enough pain in her pain in her thirty years to last a lifetime. She took a quick sip of water and rolled her head from side to side, trying to loosen the knots that had formed during her realization.

"*Determined in Fort Worth*, you're on the air with Dr. Lovegood."

"Hi, Dr. Lovegood. I really enjoy your show. I enjoy everything about you," he said, giggling. "You see, I've got a serious problem. I hope you can help me out."

The hair on the back of Eve's neck tingled at the man's voice, a sing-song voice that told her some silverware was missing out of his top drawer. "What's your problem?"

"There's this woman that I'm madly in love with. She's real smart, a doctor. I'm determined to get her to love me back," he said, his voice hard and then softening once again to a childlike quality. "How should I do that?"

Eve's throat was as dry as dust, and she looked at Lucy through the glass. It made her feel marginally better that Lucy's finger was already on the disconnect button, but she shook her head slowly, telling her to wait to sever the connection. She wanted to hear what the man had to say. She remembered the note that lay wadded at the bottom of her purse.

She'd had secret admirers before, and it always helped to have as much information as possible before going to the police. And the man didn't sound dangerous, just fixated.

"Have you told her how you feel?"

"No," he said. A high pitched laugh slithered across her skin. "I'm just at the watching stage. I watch her all the time, even when I'm supposed to be at work. I told you I'm in love with her. Do you think I should try to get her attention?"

"I think you should go about your day to day routine, including your job, and if she notices you and shows interest, that's when you should try to get her attention."

"Now, I can't do that, Dr. Lovegood. She'd never notice me. She thinks she's in love with someone else, but that's just because she hasn't gotten to know me yet. I think I'll just have to make her notice me. By the way, Dr. Lovegood, I really like your house. It has a lot of… character."

Eve cut to commercial immediately and put her head between her knees. He knew where she lived. Great. Now she'd have to watch out for a crazy admirer on top of everything else that was happening in her life.

"We have the number on caller ID. I'll go ahead and get it to the police and see if we can track him down," Lucy said, laying a comforting hand on Eve's shoulder. "It was probably a pay phone though."

"It's all right. I'll just keep my eyes open. This has happened before. I know the drill."

"Are you ready to get back at it?"

"As ready as I'll ever be."

"Good, because *Waiting in Dallas* is on the phone, and I wouldn't mind feeling my heart go pitty-pat before I go home tonight."

"He's on the phone? I can't talk to him yet. I'm not ready." Eve felt her lungs burn from holding in a breath and let it out in one loud whoosh.

"What's the matter with you? Does this have to do with the thing that's bothering you but you're not ready to talk about?"

Eve shooed her out of the room and did a few deep breathing exercises. She was a professional. A professional who was attracted to a man that was romancing her in front a couple of million people. Piece of cake.

"*Still Waiting in Dallas*, welcome back, you're on the air with Dr. Lovegood." Her breathing had slowed and was under control, and she wondered where he was calling from.

"Hiya, Doc."

"Hi yourself. What can I do for you tonight?"

Eve shivered at the sexy laugh that floated across the line, and she blushed when she realized the question could be taken two ways. "Have you come to the realization that it wasn't really love at first sight after all?"

"No, it is definitely love. The kind of love that makes me weak in the knees and makes me wants to see a glimpse of her smile every minute of every day. I just wanted to get back to what you talked about earlier, the key ingredients to a relationship."

"Yes?" she asked.

"Well, I'd like to know your professional opinion on whether or not a man should be condemned by his past. Does love, real love, deserve a clean slate for its fragile beginnings?"

She knew he wasn't going to make things easy on her.

"As a doctor, I know the right answer to the question. Yes, everyone deserves to start fresh, and if it really is love then your past shouldn't matter as long as your past truly stays in the past. As a woman, that question is harder to answer. There will be self doubt until she trusts you enough to know that what you say is the truth and will always be the truth. It's right for her to be cautious. Statistics show that it is especially difficult for men to change the dating pattern when looking for the next woman. They rarely vary their technique, especially when a man is over thirty. And when a woman has been burned in a past relationship, it's hard to change their way of thinking when involved with a man they know has a prolific history with women. What if she falls in love with you and then you break her heart? I'm not sure I…I mean…she could go through that again. For some women, love only comes once. She'll need to decide if you're worth the risk."

"And am I worth the risk?" Jake asked softly.

Eve felt a vise she recognized as panic grip her heart. "I…I don't know."

There was a charged silence across the airwaves, and Eve chanced to look up at Lucy. There were silent tears streaming down her face and everyone at the station was frozen, listening to the exchange.

"I guess I'll have to do everything I can to get her to trust me, because for some men, once they meet the right woman, all others are just a distant memory. There's something about meeting *the one*, you know what I'm saying, Doc. I knew it from the first instant. Something just clicked inside me and I knew it was meant to be. And then I touched her, and all the pieces fell into place. I won't give up on her. I'll work as hard as I have to to make her trust me. Because for me, all those other women are just a distant memory. Love only comes once, and I've found her."

Eve had never been so ready to get home to a crumbling house in her life. She'd gone through the rest of her program on autopilot, not really sure what she'd told her listeners and hoping it was good advice, whatever it was.

She almost wept in relief when she saw Jake's truck parked in her driveway, but managed to get out of the car without flinging herself into his arms. He was sitting on the tailgate of his truck, two glasses of champagne in his hands.

"Hey, Doc," he said.

It would take a stronger woman than she'd ever been for the need in his eyes to not weaken her resolve.

"Hey, yourself. Nice night." It was forty degrees and looked like it could rain at any moment, but her body temperature was so high she hardly noticed.

He laughed and handed her a glass. "Absolutely beautiful."

Eve ignored the butterflies in her stomach and accepted the glass, unsure what she should do next.

"Why don't we get this out of the way?"

Jake kept his hands still, sure she'd run like a rabbit if he touched her now, and gently lowered his lips, soft and warm, to hers. He rubbed them gently back and forth, and felt her shudder beneath him. The tension left her shoulders and her body relaxed as she leaned into the kiss. And when he heard her moan, he reached up gently to cup her face. Her mouth opened beneath his, and her surrender was more than he could have hoped for. His tongue warred with hers and she met his passion with equal fervor.

There was an ache deep inside that Eve couldn't describe. It pounded in her chest and throbbed in her loins. But the pleasure…God, the pleasure was unlike anything she'd ever experienced. She pulled him closer and let the fire burn that she'd left as embers so long ago. The hardness of his body cradled her softness, and she wanted nothing more than to lose herself in his touch.

When they parted, Eve knew her life had changed. She'd always remember him like this, the shadow of night and the glow of the moonlight, soft music and gentle hands. Hands that were patient even though she could feel the vibrations of fierce desire coursing through his body.

"There," he said, his voice husky with need. "That's better."

"I don't know if I'd go that far," Eve said, shaken.

He laughed and brought his lips to hers again briefly. "Well, I think it's something I could get used to it. Dance with me."

He turned on the stereo he'd left in the bed of his truck, and the soothing sounds of Billie Holiday floated through the air. He held out his hand, waiting for her to make the next move. When she stepped into his embrace, it was like coming home.

They moved slowly and held each other lightly, knowing what a tenuous beginning they shared. And when his lips touched hers again, everything disappeared around her, the music, the autumn air and the stars. There was only Jake, and she could feel his love bearing down on her, no matter how hard she tried to ward it off.

"I'm dizzy," she whispered.

"Me, too," he said, stopping the slow spin. "You make me want, Eve. So much that I ache from it."

"I..."

"Shh," he said, placing his finger across her lip. "You don't have to explain anything. I know we're moving at different speeds. I've got a surprise for you."

"I don't think I can take any more surprises," she said with a nervous laugh.

"Come on," he said, leading her to the back of his truck.

"Well, you've been busy," she said, eyeing the blankets and pillows.

"I thought we'd lie under the stars and talk a bit if that's all right with you. I'd like to know you, all of you."

This was the last thing Eve had expected. Talk. She was sure Jake would have tried to get her into bed at this point, and she probably would have gone with him. He obviously had a few tricks up his sleeve, and she'd have to keep on her toes to keep her heart protected.

"Okay," she said, getting into the truck bed. She accepted the hot chocolate he'd poured from a thermos and propped her back against the mound of pillows. When he settled in beside her she scooted closer, his body like a furnace on the cool night.

"Tell me your deepest, darkest secrets," he said, not so subtly putting his arm around her.

"Very smooth," she said, laughing. "Let's see, I love music from the forties, and I am deathly afraid of rodents."

"Hmm, not exactly the dark secrets I was looking for, but I can work with it. Now it's my turn. I'm an only child, with more money than I could ever spend in this lifetime because my grandmother decided to bequeath all of her money to me and my only cousin for some reason that I'll never understand, and I like to buy my boxer shorts from Wal-Mart because they're the softest. I also would love to have a dog someday. I never had one as a kid because they didn't mix well with my mother's rose garden."

"Ooh, very mysterious. Is it my turn?"

He answered her by kissing the top of her head and smoothing the wayward curls behind her ears.

"I graduated from high school two years early and completed my undergrad and graduate work by the time I was twenty. I had my doctorate by the time I was twenty-four and opened a private practice the same year. I'm what you might call a prodigy."

"Mmm…smart women really turn me on," he said, nipping the side of her jaw with his teeth. "I have an MBA that I have never used and nearly gave my parents a stroke when I told them I was going into the construction business. But, I'm very proud of the company, and they've learned to live with it and not talk about me in polite company. I believe I'm considered the black sheep of the family."

Eve thought that was a very telling statement. It hurt, no matter what age you were, to not have the approval of your parents. Hers had always been there for her. No matter what, even though she'd grown up in the same circles of the wealthy that Jake had.

"But Ruth is proud enough of you to make up for everyone else," she said, touching the side of his cheek in comfort. "Sometimes you have to do what's best for yourself, even though it might be the most difficult path to accept for others.

"Yes," he whispered. "A little bit of free therapy?" he asked, annoyed that he'd been read so easily.

"I didn't mean…I'm sorry," Eve said, putting more than just physical distance between them. *Why couldn't she ever learn to keep her mouth shut?*

Jake pulled her closer, despite her protests, and buried his face in the soft fragrance of her hair. "No, I'm the one who's sorry. It was a cheap shot, and I didn't mean it. It's just that my family has always been a raw spot with me. I've never had anyone to share it with. I've never had anyone I wanted to share it with."

Eve understood. It was as if she could look at him and see all the hurts and triumphs he'd had his entire life. No one had ever looked at him that way, not even Ruth, for she still didn't understand why he wouldn't use the money that piled up with interest in his accounts every month. He was determined to make it without the backing of his trust fund or using the connections of his parents. And he had made it. And now with Eve, his life felt complete.

"Marry me, Eve."

Her hand froze on his cheek. "What?"

"I said marry me. I love you, and I want to have a thousand nights just like this one, with you."

"Don't do this to me, Jake. It's not fair. I'm not saying you couldn't make me love you. You could. But after we have our thousand nights together, will you get bored and move on to something more exciting? Will we have a few nights of pleasure followed by a lifetime of misery? I can't marry you," she said, her voice hitching and tears burning her eyes.

He had expected some surprise, some trepidation, but he hadn't expected the fear and the bitterness in her eyes. He'd gotten carried away in the moment. He hadn't planned to propose for a few more weeks, but dammit, he loved her. Why couldn't she see that?

"Why not? Is love not enough for you? What do I have to do? I want a commitment from you, a home, a family. I'm not the person I was ten years ago looking for a different woman while still playing with the first. I want you. Forever."

"Jake, I don't want to hurt you."

"The hell with that. Tell me what you feel."

"I don't know. We've only known each other a couple of weeks. I'm not convinced that love at first sight is real. I know it's not for me. I need security and trust. Marriage is not something I've ever planned on going through again. And if you'd been there before, you wouldn't bother asking because you'd know what a miserable experience it can be. I won't marry you. I can't. I'm sorry."

Jake watched her jump out of the truck and run into the trailer. She'd been married before, and he'd had no clue. He leaned his head back and looked up at the stars. The first drops of freezing rain fell on his face and ran down his cheeks like tears.

"Perfect. Just perfect."

He put his hand on top of the ache in his chest and rubbed. *Hurt?* Hurt didn't begin to describe what he was feeling. Was love always so painful? He'd obviously miscalculated, but that just meant a change in strategy was needed. He was in love with Eve Lovegood, whether they'd known each other a few days or a few years. He was going to get to the bottom of this past marriage and then work on making her fall in love with him. He wasn't a quitter.

Jake hopped out of the back of the truck as the rain started to fall in earnest, not as heavy-hearted as he was before, but just as determined.

chapter eight

Steve Slater's wife.

Jake stared blankly at the paperwork in front of him. No wonder Eve didn't want anything to do with marriage. He remembered enough of what the gossip columns had said after his death to know that Eve hadn't had an easy time of it. He even remembered that the gossip had reached his parents circles. It wasn't everyday when one of their own was killed so tragically.

He hadn't paid much attention at the time. His business was just beginning to make it on its own, enough to where he'd made George a partner, and it was around the same time that his grandmother had fallen down a flight of stairs and ended up in the hospital for a few weeks.

Ruth had scared the hell out of him, and he'd

given her a good blistering when he'd found out she'd talked one of the neighborhood kids into lending her a sled so she could use it to ride down the imaginary mountain. She was lucky she hadn't broken anything, only a concussion and a few scrapes and bruises, but her age had slowed down the healing process. No, he'd given little thought to the death of Steve Slater, and even less of his widow. Had she grieved? Had she loved him? Those were questions that left him with guilt and jealousy, so he pushed them aside. He'd approached her all wrong. He knew that now.

He'd decided after his failed proposal that he was going to have to know all about Eve to break down her defenses. He was still spending time with her, wooing her, but he hadn't touched her intimately since that night. They'd had quiet dinners filled with laughter and conversation, and long drives filled with comfortable silences. But his need hadn't diminished. And neither had his love. If anything it was stronger than ever. He wished his lips had never touched hers and his hands had never felt her curves pressed closely to him because then he wouldn't know what he was missing. Her taste would still be a dream instead of a memory.

And after the private investigator he'd hired had delivered the stunning information about her marriage, he wasn't sure he'd be able to go through with his plan. Eve was right. She'd been through enough pain to last a lifetime. The marriage behind the scenes had been fairly quiet from the media's viewpoint, and Eve had come across as a cold wife and even colder widow. But he knew Eve. There wasn't a cold bone in her body. She was warm and generous, and she felt too much. She had just been trying to survive.

Maybe his grandmother could help him out with a few ideas on how to win the girl. She'd know better than anyone.

Jake pushed the chair back from his desk and closed the file folder. The headache that had started as a dull ache behind his eyes earlier in the day was now full-fledged, so he threw back a couple of aspirin with some Glenfiddich before hunting down his grandmother.

He looked around at his Spartan office and wondered what Eve would think about his house. He'd never really considered it a home, just a place to sleep until the next job came along or until he found the right house to settle down in with a family. He'd lived there almost ten years. It was big and spacious, with skylights and a landscaped yard, but it lacked love. It lacked Eve. He'd considered Eve's house more of a home than he ever had his own place.

He headed towards the guest rooms he'd had

furnished especially for Ruth whenever she got a wild hair and decided to come visit. He found it ironic that his parents didn't warrant their own space. They'd only been to visit once in the time he'd lived there. He was always expected to come to them, a dutiful son paying his once a year respects to two people who were so absorbed in their own lives that they couldn't be bothered to check on their only son every now and then, just to make sure he was still alive. He shook away the thoughts, knowing they'd do nothing more than add to his already pounding headache.

"Edward," he called out after not finding Ruth in any of her rooms. He headed towards the kitchen knowing that if anyone knew where Ruth was, it was Edward.

"Yes, sir." Edward came out of his own room, still dressed in crisply pleated black slacks and a white button down shirt. The man had looked the same ever since Jake had been a little boy. His silver hair was parted and neatly combed and his long, scholarly face somber with the responsibilities of caring for the very rich. Taking care of his grandmother would be no easy task.

"Do you know where my grandmother is?" For the first time that Jake could remember, Edward looked as if he wasn't sure exactly what he should say. And even more strange, the man wouldn't look him in the eyes. "What's going on Edward?"

"I believe your grandmother is spending the evening with Ms. Lovegood."

"Hmmm. What is it that they're doing that had you contemplating lying about it?"

Edward's cheeks turned a dull red under Jake's scrutiny, but not in fear for his position. When you'd walloped a boy's backside for getting into things he shouldn't, there couldn't be fear in the relationship. It was embarrassment that tinged his cheeks.

"Your grandmother mentioned taking Eve to High Pointe Lake. She said that Ms. Lovegood didn't get into near enough trouble to suit her."

"That sounds like something she'd say," Jake said, already wondering what kind of situation he was going to have to get his grandmother out of. "Any hint as to what I'm going to be walking into, Edward?"

"Not a clue, sir, but knowing your grandmother as well as I do, I'm sure it will be interesting."

Jake eyed the man curiously, "When are you going to make an honest woman out of my grandmother?"

"I beg your pardon, sir, but I'm not sure anyone could make an honest woman out of Ruth."

Jake roared with laughter and slapped the man on the back before he headed to High Pointe Lake.

He was looking forward to seeing what kind of trouble his grandmother could get Eve into.

"I don't know, Ruth. I don't think this is such a good idea," Eve said.

"Buck up, girl. If you're going to be my grand-daughter-in-law I want to see what you're made of. Now strip those clothes off before someone drives by."

"That's the thing, Ruth. I don't think I'm going to be your grand-daughter-in-law."

"Why the hell not?"

"Because I've been married before. It wasn't an experience I care to repeat. I spent the entire two years of my marriage watching my husband rub other women in my face. Jake and I haven't been to a restaurant, a picnic or a movie yet where we haven't run into one of his old girlfriends. I'm sure I'm presenting a great challenge to Jake, but in the end, when I'm no longer a challenge, he's going to go look for the next one. A woman like me doesn't hold the attention of a man like Jake for very long."

"Well, that's just plain stupid," Ruth said. "Quick. Duck!"

Eve hit the ground with a jarring thud and hoped Ruth hadn't broken anything in her quest to be invisible. She'd hate to have to explain why they were sneaking around on private property. She groaned as she sat up gently, small pebbles pressed into her knees and grass stuck to the palms of her hands.

"Come on. Let's get this done with," Ruth said, shedding her clothes in a heap on the ground.

"Ohmigod!" The sight of Ruth Murphy naked was something she'd never be able to scrub from her memory. She looked like a ninety pound soup chicken, papery skin and bony knees and elbows. Eve had never been more grateful for a night without stars.

"It's going to rain. We'll both catch a cold swimming in a freezing lake while the rain hammers at us from the other end."

"Nonsense. The rain won't be here for a while yet. Are you a fraidy cat?"

Eve heard the splash as Ruth jumped into the lake. She wasn't afraid. Well, maybe a little because it probably wouldn't be good for her career if she was caught, but she put her fears aside and stripped down. She was going skinny dipping with a woman who wanted her to love her grandson.

"This water is freezing," Eve screamed.

"Of course it is. It's December. Just because we still have the occasional eighty degree day doesn't mean the water is going to cooperate."

"Now tell me what your plan is regarding my

grandson. I know you have one."

"Well, since I turned down his proposal a few weeks ago, he's kind of kept his distance. I mean, he still sends flowers and we go out, but there's space between us. He's fun. We're having fun together," she qualified. "It's like he's decided he's happy just being my friend. We're getting to know each other and that's good, but a part of me has to wonder if he worked that hard with all his other conquests. Now I'm confused because I don't know if he still wants me that way or not. The problem is, Ruth, I could fall in love with him if I let myself."

"There's no let about it. You either are or you aren't. And if you weren't in love with him already, you wouldn't be worrying so much about all this nonsense. And Jake definitely wouldn't be spending all this time with you if he just wanted to be your friend. It's you he wants. Hell, half of this country is following your relationship with Jake on your show every night. I tune in now just so I can hear him make a fool of himself."

Ruth was right. Her ratings had skyrocketed since Jake began calling into the show. Things seemed easier, safer, when they talked over the airwaves. He was a good man. A sensitive, caring, patient man. And honorable. It was a bitter pill to swallow that she was running out of excuses to keep him at a distance.

His own self imposed distance was driving her insane, and she found herself watching him closely to see if the fire would leap between them whenever he looked at her. But though there was a sliver of hope somewhere beneath the surface, she knew that there couldn't be a future for them.

"He's a man you can be proud of, and I care for him a great deal. But I don't think I can spend the rest of my life with him, wondering, hoping that his feelings for me are real. My marriage taught me that trust was something to give sparingly, and that giving your whole heart to one person just means it hurts worse when they crush it. There's not much left of my heart, Ruth."

"Sounds like your ex-husband was a horse's patoot."

"He was, but he's not my ex-husband. I'm a widow."

The breath Ruth drew in had Eve swimming in that direction, afraid that she was having a heart attack and about to drown. "You didn't kill him did you?"

Eve stopped swimming and stared at Ruth in shock before she started laughing. "No, I didn't kill him. I was married to Steve Slater. He was very popular on the racing circuit."

"I watch the horse races. I have a right fine hand

at the windows if I do say so myself. I don't recall hearing about a Steve Slater though."

"He was a race car driver. He wrapped his car around a tree in Monte Carlo one night. The roads were slick and he'd had too much to drink. There weren't very many pieces of him or his mistress left when the car was found. I hadn't seen him in over a month. He was almost a stranger to me, and I feel guilty because all I felt was relief when he died."

"Ahh…Guilt is a powerful weapon. Even when wielded from the grave. Mistakes are meant to be learned from. One thing I've learned in my ninety years is that you can't judge a person by someone else's mistakes. It doesn't seem very fair to Jake that you'd try."

"No, but other than the fact that Jake loves all women too much to abuse them, there seem to be too many similarities for me to be fair at this point."

"It sounds like you're determined to grow old alone and miserable. I've found that's something that most people have to work pretty hard at, especially when the love is there. Maybe you deserve a good kick in the pants instead if you can't see the difference. I thought you showed promise, girl, but I'm not so sure now."

Eve wasn't sure what to say. She was embarrassed about bringing up her past and ashamed at the same time with the set down Ruth had just given her. She was about to apologize when she saw the headlights that stopped on the side of the road.

"Ruth, someone's here. What do we do?"

"Oh, drat. I hope it's not the police. Jake got quite upset the last time he had to bail me out of jail. He got that little line on his forehead like he does when he's angry, and he didn't talk to me for a whole day."

Eve thought Jake probably had a lot of patience if Ruth pulled stunts like this all the time and he still let her stay at his house. She was lucky he didn't put her in a loony bin.

"What the hell are y'all doing down there?"

Eve sighed at the familiarity of the voice. They weren't going to jail after all.

"Don't talk to us in that tone of voice, young man. I can switch your bottom just as easily now as I did when you were eight years old."

"Someone needs to switch yours," he said in response. "You could catch your death in that cold water. Didn't you learn anything when you were in that hospital a few years ago? Look at Eve's lips. They're blue."

Eve reached up and touched her numb lips aware of the fact that Jake's eyes had never left hers. She wanted nothing more than to get out of the freezing water, but reality intruded. She was naked.

"It's not nice of you to remind me about that little incident. If that sled hadn't had a warped set of runners, I would have sped right down those stairs instead of flipping over."

"You don't really want to go back there, do you, Gran?"

Jake looked like he was ready to explode, and Ruth was right, he did get a little line on his forehead when he was angry. It was everything Eve could do not to ask what happened, but she didn't want to direct any attention to herself.

"No, I suppose not. Well, I guess we're all done here. I just wanted to get Eve out of the house. You can't let her get too settled in her ways or she gets a little stuffy. Someone's got to teach the girl how to have a little fun before she ends up like a dried up old prune."

Ruth stepped out of the lake, naked as a jaybird, and went for her clothes.

"Good grief, Gran, you could have waited until I turned my back."

"Oh, pish-posh, Jake. Don't be such a prude. I know my body looks like a science experiment or one of those cadavers they cut on in medical school."

"Why me?" Jake said under his breath.

"I heard that," Ruth said, getting into his truck. "Make sure you take care of that girl."

"I plan to," he said, bringing Eve's clothes down to her.

"I don't suppose you're going to give me the same treatment," he asked, his smile rakish and disarming.

"I don't think so. I still have a ways to go before I'm as brave as your grandmother."

"Thank God for small favors. I'll have to ask about your sanity with my back turned. How could you let my grandmother talk you into something like this? You seem like a sensible woman. I was hoping you'd be a good influence on her."

Eve started to laugh so hard at that statement she could barely get out of the water. "Jake, your grandmother is old enough to make her own decisions. She doesn't need a keeper. And I sure as hell am not going to get in her way when she gets it into her mind to do something."

The sound of her clothes sliding over wet skin was driving him insane. He couldn't concentrate on what she was saying when she was naked so close behind him, so he just gave her a noncommittal hmm and turned around.

"I've missed you," he said, pulling her into his arms and kissing her with all the pent up passion and frustration he'd been holding back over the last weeks.

The cold left her body quickly and turned into a blazing inferno at the first touch of Jake's body. This is what she'd been missing through the weeks of platonic dinners and brotherly pecks. No matter what she felt about Jake's ability as a trustworthy partner, she knew she wanted him. And she knew she wanted him because she was already in love with him. Her mind would let her do no less.

"I've been wanting you to do that," she said, placing her hand upon his cheek. "I've been going crazy remembering what it was like and then making do with those horrid brotherly pats on the back."

"It hasn't been easy keeping my hands off you, but I wanted to give you space. I can't do it anymore. Let me come home with you tonight," he whispered. "I need to be with you."

Eve knew the desperation in his eyes mirrored her own. She would deal with the consequences of her decision later. Tonight, she needed him.

"Yes. Come home with me tonight."

Jake let out the breath he'd been holding, sure that she would reject him again. He wasn't going to let her get away. Before the night was over, she'd belong to him and no other.

"I'll drive Gran home and meet you at your house."

"I guess it's a good thing you finished the downstairs bedrooms."

"I had a feeling we might need one before too long. I know where to put my priorities when I build a house. Besides, I don't want to limit our activities to the bedroom. I worked overtime to make sure the kitchen and other rooms were finished in record time."

"You can't think to…"

"Oh, I can think. I plan on christening every one of those rooms. Now get a move on and stop tempting me with that wet shirt. I'm not a saint, you know."

"I've noticed that," she said, dodging him before he could grab her in another soul searing kiss.

Eve hurried to her car, as giddy as a young girl, wondering how long it would take him to get the second floor finished so they could try those rooms out as well.

chapter nine

Eve lit white tapered candles all over the bedroom. Her hands shook with nerves and pep talks were no longer doing the trick. Reminding herself that she was a grown woman who knew exactly what she was doing didn't relieve the pressure in her chest. The worry that Jake Murphy would walk away with more than she was willing to give when it was over left an ache she couldn't soothe.

She looked around the room. He'd done an amazing job with the house in the months he'd been working on it. It was sturdy, built to last, and it was hers.

The first floor was completed, the rooms painted and furnished. They'd had fun picking out colors and flooring, arguing as most couples probably would when faced with the same situation, but they weren't a couple, and Jake would leave when the project was finished. All she'd have left of him was the home they'd made together. Somehow that would be the most painful thing of all.

She hadn't had a home when she'd been married to Steve. She'd been finishing her doctorate and then starting a practice. He'd never wanted to stay where she was for very long anyway, so she'd set up an apartment to her liking and welcomed him home when he thought to stop by. Why had she settled for that kind of a relationship? She had loved Steve at one time. He'd been an exciting, dynamic knight on a white horse, and she'd been a naïve rich girl that had more use for books than sexy shoes or highlights in her hair. And she'd been lonely. Hadn't that been at the heart of it all?

And when Steve had died, there'd been no love left. He'd killed it long before he'd crashed his car so recklessly. But that was Steve, reckless, careless, selfish. It was part of his appeal, to his fans and to her, but no one knew the real Steve Slater like she had. She'd have to tell Jake eventually, but not tonight. There wasn't room for the past tonight.

She jumped when she heard the knock on the door. "Silly," she said. "There's nothing to be nervous about. It's just Jake."

Opening the front door was one of the hardest

things she'd ever done.

"Hi."

"Hi, yourself," he said, leaning his shoulder against the door frame and looking at her intently. There were flowers in his hand, white roses that she planned to fawn over when she was alone, and his hair was damp. The air smelled of rain, a gentle shower that would be gone before it had started.

"Are you going to invite me in?" Jake asked.

Wasn't that the question that would change everything? She wasn't just inviting Jake into her bed for the night. She was inviting him into a part of her soul that she thought had withered long ago.

He saw the doubt in her eyes, the denial, and knew that she could just as well turn him away for expecting too much, but he needed something. This wasn't meaningless to him, no matter how much she pretended otherwise.

"It wasn't a trick question, Eve. Invite me in. Give us a chance."

"I'd like you to come in," she said, standing back to let him in. His gaze never left hers as he crossed the threshold he'd repaired so many weeks before.

"Here, let me put those in some water," she said, looking for something desperately to do with her hands. "They're beautiful."

Jake let her have them and reminded himself to be patient. She needed something she'd never gotten from Steve Slater, but he had to tramp down his own desire to make it special for her.

"You could always change your mind, you know," Jake said, crossing his fingers. "I wouldn't want to pressure you into something that you're not ready for." He hoped lightning didn't strike him dead for that lie. He was desperate, and he'd do anything to get Eve exactly where he wanted her.

Eve snorted out a laugh. "That is such a lie. You should be careful saying things you don't mean. What if I took you up on it and invited you to play a game of Monopoly?"

"I'd tell you to get prepared to lose. My daddy taught me how to play real life Monopoly, and I play to win. Of course, we could always play a different version. Maybe the loser would have to make love to the winner."

"Hmm, I should've known you'd find some way for it to be turned in your favor. You're a sneaky man, Jake Murphy."

"That's what I'm told. Come here," he said, pulling her into his arms. "I want to do only what you're ready for, Eve. I love you."

He felt her body tense and ignored the pang it brought. "Now don't shy away from that. I'll make sure to tell you as often as possible so you can get used to it. But if you need more time, I'll give it to you, because nothing is more important to me than you are. But at the same time, I'm not going to sit by and wait patiently. I'm going to do everything in my power to persuade you to change your mind. Like kissing you," he said, dropping his lips to her forehead.

He feathered kisses over her eyelids and made his way to her ear and then down to the tender spot just below her jaw before she moaned and realized the sound had come from her.

"I could kiss you for hours."

She would forever be branded in his mind just as she was this first time. Dark curls soft around her face and her witchy eyes bright with anticipation, confusion and nerves. There were no trappings that most women he'd been with liked to use, no seductive perfume or sexy lingerie. Just Eve. That was all he needed.

Eve wondered at his gentleness when she could see the desperation and desire banked just behind his gaze. The tension drained from her shoulders at the thought that he could hold back such a fierce need for her.

He finally kissed her fully on the mouth—a tender kiss—filled with everything she'd ever longed for. He devoured her lips until he was dizzy with her scent, with her touch. The need broke through and he was frantic to touch her everywhere. They were going too fast, but he couldn't seem to pull back once the desire was unleashed.

They circled to the bedroom, and he was speechless again when he saw the dozens of candles lit around the room. Her skin glowed bronze in the candlelight and her eyes were sensuous gems. He undressed her with care—patiently—the earlier fires of desire banked with something more. And when the last of her clothes were pooled at her feet, he stood back and looked his fill.

She ducked her head in embarrassment, and her skin flushed to a rosy glow. Her breasts were full and her nipples were ripe, the color of raspberries, just waiting for him to take them in his mouth. Her waist dipped in, her hips flared out, and her legs were long and smooth. She was beautifully made, and the tightness behind his zipper was getting more painful by the moment.

"You're spectacular," he whispered. "I've never seen anything so beautiful."

Her head came up in surprise, and her eyes darkened with emotion. Hadn't anyone ever told her that before, he wondered. How could she not know how special she was?

"I want to see you too," she said, gathering her courage and stepping towards him.

Jake helped her discard his shirt then took her hands in his and held them loosely captive. "There's time enough for that, Sugar. This will end much too soon if you get your hands on me. Let me kiss you for a while. I love the way you taste."

He backed her toward the bed and followed her down on the cool sheets. He drank in her moans and gasps as she got used to the feel and weight of his body against hers. He knew she'd been married and had experienced love making before, but her reaction to him was like she was discovering the act for the very first time.

Pleasure and heat consumed his body as she matched every thrust of his tongue with her own. She fought to free her hands from his gasp, and when she did she pulled him even closer, tightening her grip on his shoulders. He kissed his way down her jaw and neck, and when he took the ripe bud of her nipple in his mouth and laved it with his tongue, it was everything her could do not to spend his seed in his jeans. Her body arched into him and her throaty purrs spurred him to find more of her sweetness.

He didn't fight her when her nimble fingers found the button of his jeans. He helped her push them down and tossed them from the bed, turning back to her arms. She took his rigid length in his hand, and her cry of surprise as he filled her hands would have fed any man's ego.

"Not yet," he chanted, holding her hands down

on each side of her body. He scraped his teeth over her belly, causing her to shiver, and placed wet kisses across her hip bones until he reached the thatch of black hair between her thighs. He could smell her arousal and see the proof of her desire between her folds. He kissed her nether lips and sought out the hidden nubbin with his tongue.

"Ohmigod," she cried. "What are you doing?"

"Loving you." So maybe she was more of a virgin than he'd thought. The thought that he could be the first to give her something filled him with satisfaction.

He swirled and flicked his tongue until she was writhing between him, on the cusp between here and oblivion. He inserted his finger inside her to the second knuckle and then curled it up, so he pressed against her most sensitive spot. She went wild in his arms, bucking against his mouth and finger as she came apart in his arms. Her cream tasted of the sweetest nectar and soaked his fingers.

"Please, please," she begged, delirious from his touch. "I don't know what you're doing to me. I can't take any more."

He moved up her body slowly, so the motion was one long sinuous caress. The tip of his cock touched her moist folds, but he didn't enter her. "I'm giving you everything I've ever dreamed of. And you can always take me. Take me," he said as he pushed inside her.

Even with her adequately prepared, the fit was still more than snug. He moved slowly and swallowed every whimper and cry with a kiss as they became one. And then he began to move, and he never wanted to be anywhere else. She wrapped her legs around his waist and clawed at his back, her hips meeting his with every thrust.

"Look at me, Eve."

Her eyes opened slumberously and she met his gaze. He felt her tighten around him and knew he wouldn't last much longer.

"This is everything, baby. I love you."

She cried out beneath him, her womb pulsing around his cock, and he gave everything he had to her as he came inside her. He collapsed on top of her, his heart pounding against his chest in the aftermath of something he'd never felt before.

Jake rolled to the side so he wouldn't crush her and pulled her close so they held each other. They were both lost in their own thoughts, afraid to move, afraid the magic would be broken.

Eve sighed and stretched her well used muscles. *So that's what she'd been missing all her life*, she thought. Incredible. No one had ever made love to her as if she was delicate—beautiful…something special. She'd treasure Jake always for that alone.

She'd had two lovers in her thirty years. The first

had been a mistake. She could admit that now without shame. What she'd felt for Steve couldn't hold a candle to what she felt for the man in her arms. But the second man who'd claimed her body…he would leave her devastated. Jake Murphy was much more lethal to her heart than Steve Slater could have ever hoped to be. There would be no other lovers after Jake. She loved him with everything she had.

"Eve…" His fingers trailed down her spine, and she felt the tingle of desire begin once more.

"Mmmm." She arched against him, loving the feel of her nipple against his chest hair.

"I think we have a problem."

Eve froze in his arms, the lust cleared from her mind with terror. God, what had she done wrong? She'd heard it often enough before. When she'd first been married to Steve, she'd heard all about the "problems" during sex. She was too aggressive. Then she wasn't aggressive enough. She expected too much. And then she learned not to expect anything but a few minutes of sweat and discomfort.

She'd been a virgin on her wedding night, but she hadn't been afraid of it. Sex was a new experience and she'd tackled it with the same determination she'd used to finish her doctorate and open her own practice. But Steve told her men didn't like for the women to take charge. When she finally learned to just lay there and take it, he'd compared her to a plastic blow up doll. After that, she hadn't cared one way or another, because he'd found other women to fulfill his needs.

"What...What did I do wrong?" she finally asked. She loved Jake enough to try and fix whatever it was. This was the first time after all. There was plenty of time to practice. Surely they'd get better.

Jake realized she was serious. Her eyes were hurt and unshed tears rested on her lashes. He wiped his thumb gently at the corner of her eye and caught a tear.

"Don't ever compare me to him, Eve. I would never hurt you. I love you. I was going to say we have a problem because I'm going to want to do this often. Probably everyday. More than once. Do you think you can handle that?"

She laid her lips against his, with a kiss that held all the love she felt for him.

"I could probably get used to it," she choked out with a laugh.

She would live in the moment, she assured herself. What more could happen besides getting her heart broken?

chapter ten

The explosion rocketed through the established neighborhood sometime after midnight, and Eve heard the tinkling of glass as it hit the wood floor in one of the front rooms.

"My windows," she said, getting out of bed and throwing a robe on. Jake was already a step ahead of her and had his jeans pulled on and a pair of sneakers on his feet.

"Let's go," he said, pulling her by the arm. "I want you to stay close until we can figure out what the hell is going on."

"What was that? It sounded like the whole neighborhood was destroyed. Do you think it was a gas line?" She bumped into Jake's back when he stopped suddenly.

"No. It was the trailer," he said, looking at what

was left of his office. Fortunately, he hadn't had anything important inside. He'd let Eve have the run of it during working hours since her own office inside the house wasn't finished yet.

"Oh, no," Eve said. "My work. It's all gone." She ran out the front door in her bare feet, hoping to salvage something of the papers that were flying down the street.

"Eve, wait," Jake said, grabbing her hand. There was glass, metal and other debris scattered everywhere, and Eve's feet were still bare. There's nothing we can do but wait for the fire department to get here."

She stopped beside him and realized she could hear the sound of sirens close by. Neighbors were all standing out on their lawns in various stages of dress. Dr. Gardener was fully clothed, just in from the hospital it looked like, and Mrs. Hansen was in a silk peignoir with a fur collar and matching slippers.

Mr. Panamaker was back on his front lawn, this time in striped pajamas. He sent her a sympathetic smile that probably had more to do with the courtside tickets to the Dallas Maverick's she'd given him as an apology than with anything else. He was probably hoping she'd go off the deep end again so he could score hockey tickets.

But Jake was steady beside her, his arms around

her in comfort and protection as she watched the violence of the flames. It wasn't too long before she started to laugh, big, gasping guffaws that bent her body over to the knees.

Jake looked at the woman he loved with concern, pulling her close and trying to comfort as best as he knew how.

"It's okay, Eve. We'll figure out something. I'll help you get caught up and sort through everything. Just think, more letters than ever will come in. You'll see, it'll be all right."

"It's perfect. Just perfect," Eve said on a hiccup. "I don't want to salvage anything. This must be fate. I was waiting for a sign."

Jake looked at her like she was a couple of sandwiches short of a picnic and that made her laugh harder. "I'm not hysterical. I promise," she added, when he looked like he wanted to argue. "But I think I've made up my mind about writing future articles for the newspaper. I'll just tell my editor that everything exploded and to find a new columnist. It's not like he can argue with me. Now I can focus on my book."

Uh, huh," Jake said with an indulgent tone, smoothing fly-a-way curls. "That's a great idea, honey. We'll need to talk to the police. Why don't you go put some clothes on? I wouldn't want them to see what a lucky guy I am with you walking around in your bathrobe."

Jake barely had time to catch her before she launched herself in his arms.

"You are the sweetest man," she said, giving him a smacking kiss before untangling herself to go get dressed. He'd been called a lot of things in his life, and he was pretty sure that sweet hadn't ever been one of them, but he could get used to it if it made Eve's smile light up like a kid on Christmas morning.

Detective Rosenberg looked like a character she'd read about in a book once, small of stature but abundant in tenacity. His clothes were disheveled and his grey hair was finger-combed and sticking up in different directions. He smelled of coffee and stale cigarettes, and her imagination gave him three ex-wives and a two pack a day habit. But underneath it all he was still a cop. He held a little notebook in his hand and his pen had leaked so it left a blue stain on the front pocket of his shirt. He looked as if he'd just gotten out of bed, which, Eve thought, looking at the clock, he probably had.

"Would you like some coffee?" Eve asked, already headed to the kitchen to complete the chore before he could answer. She need to keep busy so her mind wouldn't keep wondering what could have happened if the trailer had exploded in the daytime instead of the middle of the night. Someone could have been killed.

There were teams of people tramping around her front yard, and she guessed she should be grateful Jake's company hadn't gotten to the landscaping stage yet because everything would be ruined. There was blistered wood on the front of the house and her front windows had been broken from the blast, but nothing that couldn't be fixed. They were lucky no one had been hurt. If it had happened a few hours later, she or Jake would have been inside, oblivious and more than likely, obliterated.

She brought the coffee back in with unsteady hands.

"Sit down, love," Jake said, pulling her down beside him on the sofa, not realizing the endearment he'd let slip, but Detective Rosenberg noticed.

It was his job to assess the situation with a critical eye and his eyes told him something strange was going on. The explosion in that trailer wasn't an accident, but it was obvious that the couple in front of him had money, so that likely motive was out. They were obviously lovers, easy touches here and there, looks that were more clear than entire sentences. He'd never had much luck with the institution himself, but he could recognize it when it was staring him in the face.

"I'd like to ask you a couple of questions, Dr. Lovegood."

"Yes, of course. I don't know how much I can help you though."

"Where were you at the time of the explosion?"

A pretty blush tinged her cheeks and he thought that strange for someone purported to be one of the leading experts on relationships in the country.

"I was sleeping. I woke as soon as I heard the blast, put on some clothes and went to see what had happened, just like everyone else in the neighborhood."

"Did you see anyone you didn't recognize?"

Eve thought back to her perusal of her neighbors and shook her head. She'd recognized them all, just from their habitual comings and goings everyday, even though she hadn't been living there for long. "No, no one."

"Can you think of anyone that might want to get your attention, Dr. Lovegood? Maybe one of your husband's fans?"

Jake felt Eve stiffen as memories of her dead husband joined them in the room. He was always between them, but that was something he was determined to change.

"Doubtful," Eve said. "His fans would have more luck getting the attention of his family or his friends if that's what they wanted. I was never bothered much by them, even when he was alive."

Detective Rosenberg made a humming noise in the back of his throat that could have been construed as sympathetic or curious while he flipped through his notebook.

"I have a note here that you received a call on your talk show the night of October twenty-fifth from an infatuated fan. Is this correct?"

"What?" Jake asked, looking at Eve. "When did this happen?" Why didn't you tell me, he added silently.

Every inch of color drained from Eve's face as she thought of the caller and then the occasional notes and phone calls she'd gotten at home over the past weeks. They'd never seemed threatening so she hadn't reported them.

She looked at the anger and disappointment in Jake's face and knew she'd made a mistake, but she couldn't think about that now. She was at least able to give him eye contact when she answered him. Now wasn't the time to cower.

"He was the caller directly before you the second time you called in to the show. You wouldn't have heard the broadcast if you were on hold. And I didn't think it was that big of a deal at the time, so I didn't mention it."

"Not a big deal?" he asked, his voice level, but the anger still there.

"Have there been any other incidents?" Detective Rosenberg asked. He wanted to head them off at the pass before a domestic argument could ensue. He had enough things to deal with at the moment.

Eve hesitated before she answered, afraid of what Jake would think. "Yes. A few." She ignored Jake as he swore and got up from the couch to pace, keeping her gaze level with the detective's.

"I received a note that was left on the windshield of my car and a letter that was left in the mail box. There have also been a couple of phone calls. I wrote down what he said as soon as he started talking. I'll get everything for you. I kept them all." She made a path around Jake to pull open a drawer in the Secretary she kept near the front door and retrieved a few small pieces of paper.

How could she be so cool? Jake thought. He was furious that someone would deliberately try to hurt her, and he'd do whatever it took to protect her. But it didn't look like she wanted or needed his help. Eve Lovegood was a woman used to taking care of herself. How long would he have to hide his own hurt at her lack of trust?

"Before you ask why I didn't come to you

sooner," Eve said, "I'll tell you that this isn't the first time a fan has become a little overzealous. I know the drill. There's really nothing you could have done with a few non-threatening notes."

"You're right, Dr. Lovegood, but I wouldn't exactly call this guy non-threatening now. Would you?"

"No. This was definitely unexpected. I'll be careful. There are guards at the station and plenty of workers around here in the daytime." She didn't think about the nights. Would Jake still want to stay with her after all this? "I'll let you know if I get anything else."

"I'd appreciate that," Detective Rosenberg said, as he rose and made his way to the door. Another night of sleep lost. No wonder he couldn't stay married. He wondered if the doctor could give him a hand and then dismissed it. Who had the time? He might as well go into the station and start the paperwork. He'd leave love to the younger generation.

Eve closed the door behind the detective and turned to face Jake. She went to him before he could say anything. She could feel the war raging inside of him and only meant to soothe as best she could.

"I'm sorry, Jake." She went to him before he could say anything and laid her fingers gently over his lips. "No, please, don't say anything yet. I am sorry. I know I owe you explanations, about my marriage and what's been happening between us, but I'm just asking for a little bit more time. My feelings for you frighten me. And now this…insanity on top of everything else. I'm scared, Jake. Please don't go yet. I know you're angry with me, but please don't leave me tonight."

"Eve, look at me," he said, tilting her chin up with the tip of his finger. "I am never going to leave you. Love is not just for a little while, it's forever. Yes, I'm angry, but I'll give you a little time. I expect some explanations. I need to know you, all of you."

"Please make love with me. I need you again. I don't think I can stop shaking."

No woman should have such power over a man, but he was helpless to do but what she asked. He needed her just as desperately. If someone would have told him five years ago, hell, one year ago, that he'd fall like a ton of bricks for a sorceress with a fragile nature he would have laughed himself silly and said that Jake Murphy would bend himself for no women. He'd have been dead wrong.

He kissed her deeply, his body responding

instantly, remembering their earlier encounter with fondness.

Eve pulled his shirt from his jeans and ran her hands over the hard planes of his chest. Everything about Jake was a marvel to her, his body, his stubbornness and the innate goodness that made the core of the man.

They spoke through gestures, gentle touches and frantic kisses as he pulled her legs around his waist and entered her were they stood. He pumped into her with short, sharp thrusts and swallowed her cries of ecstasy. His knees threatened to buckle and he moved blindly to the wall and anchored her against it.

"More, more," she moaned. "I need you."

He moved his hand between them and plucked at the hidden nub between her folds. She spasmed around him and tightened like a vise as she found fulfillment. He gave a final thrust and followed her.

He propped his hand against the wall to keep them both upright until his senses came back. He carried her back to the bedroom, still intimately joined, and followed her down to the bed.

Questions would be answered later, but for now they were content. In the quiet aftermath of the storm, sleep finally found them.

chapter eleven

E ve should have realized that the explosion from the previous night would draw her back into the limelight. It had been so long since she'd been there for reasons other than her show that she'd let up her guard.

She wrapped her frigid hands around the coffee mug in front of her and looked out the front window of her breakfast nook without really seeing. The crews were already at work and the trailer had been carted away by the police. Other than the black residue that lined the street and sidewalk, there was nothing to indicate any unusual activity— other than the newspaper that had been delivered first thing that morning.

She stared at the front page photo of herself and cringed.

Steve Slater's Widow Shocked By Late Night Explosion.

"Bastards," she whispered, reading about her past in print. There was more about her marriage than there was on the actual explosion. She knew, after working around media types for the last several years, that the story was what was important. And boy did they capture the story.

The widow of the late Steve Slater, sensation of the NASCAR circuit, was startled out of sleep by an explosion that destroyed a construction trailer sitting outside of her Dallas home, which is currently being renovated by Murphy-Madsen Construction.

Dr. Eve Lovegood, host of a popular radio show, was purportedly served with divorce papers mere hours before her husband's death. There had been speculation for months about their separation when Slater began appearing in public with Gianna DeCosta, an Italian Supermodel and the daughter of billionaire tycoon Giorgio DeCosta. Miss DeCosta perished with Slater in a crash in Monte Carlo on Christmas Eve five years ago.

His widow reportedly received the inheritance from Slater's vast estates, despite the objection of his family. Dr. Lovegood couldn't be reached for comment.

Eve felt sick to her stomach. She hadn't gotten

away from the misery that Steve Slater had brought her after all.

Jake stood just inside the doorway to the kitchen and watched Eve for a few minutes. There was a lot on her mind, he knew. It seemed like her carefully constructed life was unraveling right before her eyes. He'd given her the night, but he was ready for the answers he needed. Maybe someday she'd understand that the load was lighter when two people shared the burden.

"Good morning," he said softly.

Eve turned her head in surprise and splashed coffee on the top of her hand. Jake guessed it wasn't hot since she didn't seem to notice the accident. Her face was red in embarrassment and her eyes held a fascinating combination of wariness and heat.

He walked over to her slowly and took her face between both hands before kissing her softly. The tension left her shoulders, but the heat was still there. "I said good morning," he said again.

"Good morning," she said, leaning in just once more before she could talk herself out of it. "Did you sleep well?" she asked before realizing what that implied.

Jake threw back his head in laughter when her face grew even brighter at the slip. Her innocence was refreshing. "No, I didn't sleep well at all. I hope you didn't either."

She finally relaxed and returned the smile. "No, I don't suppose I did."

"I talked Gran into visiting a friend for a few days to keep her from getting in the middle of the investigation. She watches a lot of CSI and thinks she has their secrets figured out. I knew we'd both be occupied with other things, and she has a tendency to get into trouble when left on her own."

Eve smiled absentmindedly and continued looking out the window. She looked lost.

"Have you had breakfast?" Jake asked, making himself at home and rummaging through drawers and cabinets looking for something edible. It was all so normal, like they'd been going through the routine for years.

"No. Jake, I need to tell you about…things. If you'll listen."

"I'll listen," he said breaking eggs into the sizzling pan on the stove. "Tell me about your parents. Gran tells me she knows them quite well. Your father is Dwight Lovegood?"

"Yes," she answered, smiling.

There was love there, he thought. It was hard of him to think of the tough as nails oil baron and Texas Senator that he read about in the papers as a doting father.

"I had an amazing childhood. I was very lucky. I

had all the advantages I could ask for and two parents that loved me. The only thing I was ever dissatisfied about was that they never gave me a brother or sister to play with. My mother told me that as much as she loved me, not even she would go through childbirth again just so I could have a sibling."

Jake felt the envy rising over something he'd never experienced. Despite everything, they had more in common than he once thought. He'd been neglected by his family, and she had been neglected by the man who'd promised to love and cherish her if everything he'd heard about Steve Slater was correct. He put a plate of eggs, bacon and toast in front of her and then took the seat across from her in the nook.

"I never eat breakfast," she confessed looking at the pile of food.

"You should. It's the most important meal of the day. Besides, you need to keep your energy up. You didn't get much rest last night."

Eve picked up her fork and dug in, unsure where to pick up her story. "Like I said, my childhood was great, but when I reached my teenage years I think my parents weren't sure what they should do with me. I was a child with an adult's mind who'd surpassed classmates and tutors both. I was sent to college, but I still lived at home. I remember hating that first semester because I still didn't have my driver's license and our driver had to take me everyday. It was just the beginning of a very lonely period in my life. I didn't have friends my age and didn't get the opportunity to go to parties or rock concerts. I had afternoon luncheons and committees interspersed with my studies while I finished my undergrad and then graduate work. Could I have some more coffee?" she asked, her throat dry and her palms damp.

He handed her a full cup and she waited until she thought her courage was as high as it could be before continuing. She gave him a grateful smile for being patient, for listening, just as she'd asked.

"I met Steve a couple of years after I'd started my doctoral program. It was the off season and he was in town visiting friends. We both happened to be at the same function one night, he in his tuxedo and me in an evening gown. It was like a fairytale. I was twenty-two years old and he was thirty."

Jake's gut clinched in anger. Thirty was old enough to know better than to seduce an innocent young woman.

"He walked right up to me, handed me a glass of champagne and told me how glad he was that I'd changed my mind and decided to show up, just like we'd known each other our whole lives. I was spellbound. We were the last couple on the dance floor. It was the beginning of a whirlwind courtship, and we were married a week later. I was a virgin on my wedding night," Eve said, finally looking Jake in the eye. "I haven't been with anyone else until last night."

Possessiveness clawed inside him and it was everything he could do to not go to her and hold her. To tell her that she didn't need to say anything more.

"The first three months of our marriage were amazing. We traveled all over the world. I put my dissertation on hold because I was so caught up in being married. Then the season started. I wasn't prepared for the grueling schedule."

"Steve was focused on the race, every race, and that's what he should have been focused on, but I felt like my world had just been yanked out from under me. We fought horribly, and he told me that I was just a naïve daddy's girl that didn't realize the world didn't revolve around me. I apologized to him and gave him the space he needed to win. Because winning was what was important. I came back home with the excuse of my schoolwork and being tired of the travel for anyone who asked."

Jake's eyes were dark and patient. She wanted to get up, move away, so she wouldn't feel like she should rely on the easy acceptance and support he offered unselfishly. But she stayed seated because it was important to finish it all and look him in the eye at the same time.

"He came home almost a month later as if nothing had ever happened. He was only going to be in town three days so we should make the most of it, he said. I'd missed him and I felt guilty for putting pressure on him when he should be thinking about the race, so I didn't say anything. I welcomed him home. We didn't leave the apartment for the entire three days, and then one morning he was gone. He'd packed his things and cleared out without saying goodbye. I saw him a week later on the news after he'd won the Daytona.

"That was a pattern we developed, and I didn't see anything wrong with it. I didn't want to see anything wrong with it," she clarified. "Then I saw the first tabloid. The woman was from old English aristocracy and the pictures of them kissing and coming out of their hotel arm in arm made sure the world knew they were involved romantically. I was horribly embarrassed. Mostly because I didn't want my family to know. My mother called and told me what she wanted to do to him and I just started to cry. When had I become such a wimp? I look back and realize I'd just never grown up. I was still a child in so many ways."

"It was nothing you did wrong, Eve. It was his mistake."

"A little bit of free therapy," she asked, not unkindly, mimicking his words from a night not so long ago. She pushed little bits of food around on her plate to keep her hands busy.

"It was his fault," she said. "But we'd developed a pattern. It's one of the first things you learn in psychology, behavioral patterns and human nature. I should have recognized the signs. When he came home the next time I asked him about the pictures. He gave me some song and dance about the media always making more out of things than there really was, denying the whole business. We were yelling, and the next thing I know I just pounced. I knew he was lying to me. I wanted him to realize that I could satisfy him as well as any woman. Better. I wanted proof that he still desired me, even though I knew he was lying. He never complained or fought me off during the act. God, I was almost violent. In fact, he was different than I'd ever seen him. He wasn't the gentle lover that I was used to, but he treated me like a woman. He took me with a ferocity that frightened me and excited me. When we were through he told me that men didn't like for their wives to act like common whores. He left me half dressed on the floor, grabbed his clothes and left."

The only reaction Jake showed was a tightening at the corners of his mouth. He'd loved her since the beginning, burned with passion for her through the night and still wanted her with an intensity that frightened him. Steve Slater be damned. If the man had still been alive he would have taken care of him himself.

"He changed you," Jake said.

"Yes, to a point. I was no longer a girl. I'd been introduced to adulthood the hard way. With one sentence he made me self conscious and cautious. I never trusted him again from that point. I just accepted. I raced through my dissertation with amazing speed and a focus that couldn't be interrupted by anything. I fed my sorrows with bean burritos and Hostess cupcakes and gained twenty pounds with equal determination. There were other tabloid pictures and news stories. I didn't care. At that point we'd spent more time apart than we had together. I saw him occasionally. He'd come in and take me wherever I stood, not even bothering to undress all the way, and then be off again. He was angry. At me. At himself. He wanted a reaction, and I never gave him one."

Eve took a deep breath. She had to get it all out at once before she crumbled. Things were only going to get harder, the shame and embarrassment she felt at having to bare this part of herself to Jake would make sure of it.

"There was a part of me that just withered and

died. This wasn't the man that I remembered from early in our marriage. He'd accused me of being a whore, so I decided that no involvement was better than that accusation. I'd just lay there. That infuriated him, so he'd add a slap across the face or an elbow in the ribs to see if he could get me to cry out."

Jake felt helpless, cursing himself for demanding the answers she was giving him. He didn't know how to help, how to soothe such a vicious caricature of what had been beautiful between them the night before.

She didn't even notice the tears that streamed silently down her cheeks. She was reliving her own private hell. She took another deep breath and continued, her voice empty of emotion.

"A month before he died, I was standing in the bathroom about to get in the shower. He'd left the day before and bruises were already forming on my ribs and arms. There were raised welts on my thighs where I'd been pinched. I saw myself in the mirror and didn't recognize the woman there anymore. I was a stranger, and it wasn't anyone's fault but my own."

"That's not true," Jake demanded harshly. "It wasn't your fault. It was a man's fault. A man who was old enough to know how he should treasure the precious gift that you are. It was his shortcoming and his sickness that made you a different person."

"I know that, now," she said softly. "I was ashamed. My family didn't know what to do for me. I'd put on such a convincing act, you see. I called my mother and she came over and gave it to me," Eve said smiling for the first time since she'd started. "She told me she didn't raise her daughter to be any man's punching bag and scandal be damned. How much good was I going to do people with my fancy degree if I was as sick inside as they were?"

"I think I like your mother," Jake said, rubbing his lips over the top of her hand in a gentle gesture, needing to soothe them both.

"She'd like you, too. She went with me to the attorney's office and I filed for divorce that day. I felt as if a load had been lifted. His family was scandalized, of course. They're very old money. I believe your family is connected with them."

"Yes. They probably suit each other very well. Old money, snobbish tendencies and a disdain for controversy."

"Yes, well I received an enlightening phone call from Steve's mother, demanding that I reconsider. Everyone has to deal with infidelity, she told me. It's not grounds for divorce. It was my duty to produce Steven Bixby Slater III and let Steve live his own life. I couldn't bring myself to tell her the other things. It was humiliating enough for my own family to know. I told her I wouldn't change my mind and hung up the phone."

"Good for you."

"Yeah, that was a piece of cake compared to what I'd been through already. A month later I received a phone call from the emissaries in Monte Carlo telling me that Steve was dead. I heard that he'd also killed his mistress on the news that night. The news came as a surprise to me, the same as it did with everyone else in the world. I was numb. I felt like a bystander on the outside of a glass wall looking in. We were still legally married, but he'd stopped being my husband long before. It was a hell of a Christmas. It's the reason I started doing my Christmas Eve show, so I wouldn't have to think about how empty the holiday can be. Anyway, I went to his funeral and the media decided I was a heartless gold digger because I didn't break down into hysterics like his groupies. He'd already killed everything inside of me. I had nothing left to give him."

Jake pulled on her arm until she'd moved around the table and he could shift her into his lap. He felt her pain and confusion of wondering why she'd been deemed the guilty party when she'd been the victim. An innocent bystander. A matter of circumstance. She'd built her life carefully, brick by brick, after Steve Slater's death. She was an admirable and courageous woman with a great capacity for love. He had no idea what to do.

"It's all right, Eve. Let it go," Jake said, softly. "I'll carry the burden for you."

She broke. Great gasping sobs that were wrenched from the very core of her. He offered no words of comfort, but gathered her closer and let her ride out the storm of tears. How could one person hold so much anguish inside for so long? All he could do was hold her and hope that in the end there would be peace and healing.

chapter twelve

The autumn air turned to an unexpected winter freeze the second week of December. The scent of snow was thick in the air, but the ground was still too warm for any flurries to stick.

The house, Eve was told, would be finished by the first of the year. Even now, they were working on purely aesthetic aspects and not structural changes. It was everything she'd ever wanted…and more than she could live with.

It hurt to realize she was going to have to sell it. Living in a house that carried so many memories of Jake would only be a punishment for her cowardice. He was already starting to pull away.

Life had gone on, much to Eve's complete mortification, after she'd fallen apart in his lap. For a week she'd been wined and dined, taken on romantic walks and loved tenderly in the evenings when the night could cloud the memories of her stupidity. But he watched her with a look in his eye that she could never pin down. There was a distance between them now that had never been, even when she hadn't wanted anything to do with him.

Her parents had been out of town for Thanksgiving, so they'd spent the day together, gorging themselves on the feast that Gretchen had provided, drinking champagne and falling into bed delirious with love. They'd gone shopping for antiques and seen movies and fallen into bed again. The passion between them only grew stronger as time went on, and she knew it would make life that much harder when it was time for the inevitable separation. The awkwardness from that day in the kitchen was still thick between them.

She knew life was full of changes. Expected it even. She'd resigned her position with the paper and started work full time on her book. The radio show was more popular than ever, and the week before Christmas they would begin reruns of previous broadcasts until she gave her annual four hour special on Christmas Eve from eight to midnight. But it was hard to accept the changes between them because she knew, without a doubt, that she was in love with Jake Murphy.

There had been no more letters or attention getting gestures from her admirer, or she guessed since he'd blown up some of her property that maybe he didn't admire her as much as she'd first thought. She'd almost gotten to the point where she didn't check over her shoulder every few minutes. She thought the anticipation of something bad happening was much worse than the actual letters had been.

Her picture was constantly dredged up in the newspaper, rehashing her life with the charming and talented Steve Slater. There was a new story on her every day, from her personal life married to a celebrity, the fact that she was being stalked and speculation on her new relationship with Jake Murphy, son of the Pennsylvania millionaire John Murphy. Even some of her callers had started asking personal questions about her life. In other words, it was hard to put her life with Steve Slater in the past where it belonged and focus on any chance of a future with Jake.

Jake had gotten into the habit of following her to the station, and he had talked to the security guard personally to make sure she made it to her car safely every night. Everything was so polite between the two of them. Almost too polite. She knew he was trying to protect her, to keep her from any future pain, but they weren't being themselves, and she missed their arguments. They had things they needed to talk about. An understanding they had to come to. She had to be an adult about this. She was willing to give him her love for as long as he wanted it. And she'd be content with that much. Or she'd damn well give the illusion.

Her love for Jake wasn't a girl's love as it had been when she'd married Steve. It was a woman's love. Filled with bouts of joy so full she felt she'd overflow with them, followed by pockets of heartache so intense she couldn't understand how true love could be healthy for anyone.

Eve threw the letters she'd been trying to read all morning on the desk and stood up to pace.

She'd chosen the west wing tower for her office. The octagonal room was complete, soft blues and creams contrasted with dark cherry wood furniture and scattered rugs on the newly refinished hardwood floor. Paintings that she and Jake had found at a gallery on one of their forages into the city were splashes of color on the pale walls.

It was elegant and beautiful, she thought, as she looked around in pride and frustration. She hadn't gotten one bit of work done since she'd come up earlier that morning after Jake had left the house to check on a few other jobs. Her mind had been focused on him. They were practically living together.

"Men," she huffed out, irritated at the constant distraction. "Nothing but trouble."

She gave up on doing anything productive and went downstairs to see what Gretchen had stocked in the refrigerator. She should have known that Jake would charm the woman into always having a meal ready for him. His appeal was hard to resist by any woman, young or old.

She'd barely gotten started when the back door slammed open, startling a scream out of her and wondering if she should grab a knife from the butcher block or take cover under the table.

"Whew, it's cold enough to freeze the balls off a brass monkey out there," Ruth declared through several layers of red scarf that wrapped around her entire head.

"Can you believe this weather? Last year I had the air conditioning on at Christmas. I'm surprised the earth doesn't explode into little bits of matter with all this hot, cold, hot, cold. I think I'll have my ashes shot into space. What do you think about that dear?"

"Umm...Ruth?" Eve asked, not sure that the whirling dervish under several layers of wool was really Ruth Murphy.

"Of course it's me, girl," she said unwrapping herself. "Jake, get those things in here so I can show Eve her present," she said, yelling out the door.

"You got me a present?" Eve asked, touched at her thoughtfulness.

"What have you got in these bags, Gran? You weren't gone long enough to shop this much," Jake asked, struggling to get the bags to the kitchen table.

"It's payback for shipping me off when all the action was here. Don't think I didn't realize what you were doing. I didn't even get to see the wreckage up close before you had me carted away."

Jake looked up at Eve and rolled his eyes. It always took a few minutes to adjust to the fast paced way of life that Ruth seemed to do everything in, so Eve didn't notice the woman's shrewd stare when Jake came over and kissed her gently on the forehead.

"Well, I guess it's a good thing I caught the Greyhound back here."

"You rode a bus on the way here?" Eve asked, eyes wide in surprise, imagining any number of things that could happen to a ninety year old woman who wore a three thousand dollar watch on her wrist.

"Oh, yes," Jake said, giving his grandmother a dirty look. "I got a call from Edward, who was on his way back after he arrived at her friend's house, and discovered she'd already left. I found her standing on the corner at the bus station giving tips on sexual techniques to a couple of prostitutes."

"I think those girls were new. They didn't seem to know very much." Ruth threw her coat on the counter and collapsed in a chair. "My feet hurt like the dickens."

"Did you have a nice visit with your friend?" Eve asked, putting coffee on. Sometimes it was hard to remember that Ruth was as old as she was.

"It was all right, I guess. I stayed at my friend Lorena Watkins house. She's the only one still alive that remembers me when I was beautiful, so I like to stay in touch. But I don't think I'll be visiting her for long periods of time anymore. All she could talk about was burial plots and how it was thievery to take dead people's money that way. Depressing as hell. Anyway, I had a dream last night that I was needed here," Ruth said like it was a totally reasonable explanation to do what her dreams told her to. "And I can see I'm not a moment too late. Young people have a way of messing up things that should be so simple."

"Gran," Jake said in warning.

"Well, it's obvious the two of you finally did the deed. And you must be doing it right, and I assume you are since you're a Murphy," Ruth said with a critical look. "She's got roses in her cheeks and love in her eyes. I haven't felt this much sexual tension in a room since I had that affair with that Spanish Count in 1950. He was so romantic. I've always had a soft spot for foreign royalty."

"Hmmm," Eve said, unsure what Emily Post's protocol was in situations like this one.

"But like I said, I can tell y'all are screwing this up. I'd like a great-grandchild to bounce on my knee next Christmas. You wouldn't want to deny an old woman's dying wish, would you?"

"Eve's a little gun shy," Jake said, making Eve's mouth drop open in surprise. "I'm being patient before I ask her to marry me again. Besides, it's not good for a man's ego to be turned down too many times."

"Well, don't be too patient. If I had to wager a guess, I'd say not all the hesitation is on one side," she said, making Jake frown. "I've got a sixth sense when it comes to romance. Maybe I could be a guest on your show one night, Eve."

"Maybe," Eve said, noncommittally, pretty sure that America wasn't yet ready for Ruth Murphy. She also wasn't entirely sure how she felt about her love life being discussed in the kitchen so casually.

"Now open your present," Ruth said shoving a package across the table before Eve could think too much.

Eve was expecting a completely outrageous gift, from anything along the lines of a stuffed llama to a gaudy handbag, and she already had her smile in place so Ruth wouldn't be offended. But when she unwrapped the tissue a surprised gasp escaped.

"Ruth, it's the most beautiful thing I've ever seen," Eve said tracing a finger over the delicate colored glass. The bowl was purely ornamental and unnecessary. She loved it. It was a pale blue crystal etched with gold leafed dancing ladies. "It'll be perfect for my office."

"I thought so when I came across it," she said, squeaking when Eve pulled her into a bone jarring hug. "Watch it girl. I'll snap like a twig."

"I'll show you what she got for me later," Jake said with a leer. "It's not meant for public display."

Eve laughed as he knew she would and the sound lightened his heart. She hadn't had the opportunity to laugh enough in his opinion.

"Well at least you got all your Christmas shopping done," Eve said pointing to the bags.

"Those aren't Christmas gifts. I haven't even started that mess yet. Those are all for me. I found this little lingerie shop while I was away that just had the most amazing stuff. It's the same place I found your gift, Jake."

Jake colored at the thought of what was in those bags and then decided deleting the entire memory out of his head was the best course of action.

"I tell you, my friend Lorena is not nearly as fun

as she used to be. We'd do the darndest stuff together when we were younger, dropping pumpkins from high places to hear the explosions and dressing up like candy stripers to scope out the hot doctors at the hospital, but I thought she was going to fall out of her wheelchair when I walked into that place. You'd think the woman had never had a sensuous moment in her life."

Probably not in the last forty years, Eve thought with a smile.

"Now, I'm tired. I need a nap before dinner, so tell me which room is mine. I've decided to move myself in with you since I like this place better anyway and all the action seems to be here. I told Edward he could stay at Jake's house. The man is such a worrier," she said as an afterthought.

"You're…you're staying here?" Eve stuttered.

She could feel Jake's laughter shaking his body next to her and wondered how he'd feel with her elbow in his ribs. Apparently Ruth made her own book of etiquette as she went along because it didn't look like she felt the least bit guilty inviting herself for an extended stay.

"Only through Christmas. I've got to work up the nerve to go visit my sons before the first of the year. I'll never understand how I could have given birth to two such boring men."

"I'll put you in the downstairs guest room," Eve

finally said.

chapter thirteen

"Jake, this is ridiculous. You don't have to drop everything you're doing to follow me to work. I'm perfectly safe. I haven't gotten so much as a note or a prank phone call in weeks."

"That doesn't mean he's not still out there. Have I ever told you how sexy you look in those skirts?" he asked, changing the subject. "Dr. Lovegood, professional, untouchable and legs that are smooth as silk. The whole package drives me absolutely crazy."

"You're crazy, period," she said, though the compliment pleased her. She'd spent the day doing promotional shoots at the radio station's TV affiliate and wasn't going to have time to change before heading to the station to do her program. She was already dreaming of a glass of wine and shoving her pantyhose down the disposal.

"Let's go, then," she said resigned..

"Your enthusiasm is bubbling over."

"Just like a plugged toilet," she said with a grin. She couldn't remember the last time she'd had such a carefree moment, especially with a man.

"I have an idea," Jake announced, ignoring her sarcasm.

"There is nothing in my contract about you having ideas. You're only supposed to fix my house."

"Stop being such a smart ass and listen. Besides, I think I fixed more than your house." He gave her a lecherous grin.

"Fine, fine. What's your idea?"

"I've never seen where you work."

"So what? I've never built a set of bookcases. That's why we each have our respective careers, and thank God we're good at them. You wouldn't want to see any attempt I made at carpentry."

"I'm not saying I want to go on the air, Eve. I just wouldn't mind if you invited me in to see you in action so to speak. I have all these erotic images of you when I hear your voice over the radio. I bet it would be even better if I could see you."

"You're hopeless."

Eve thought it over for a minute. "Fine. This way I don't have to deal with your nightly phone call. I'm telling you, some men just can't take a hint."

Eve barely avoided the swat to her backside that Jake aimed her way, and her laughter caused her to miss his determined smile. There was nothing he liked better than a challenge.

"I think you're going to have to get a car I can fit in," Jake said, looking at the tiny contraption and already wincing at the thought of his cramped legs.

"I'm not going to buy a new car so you can be comfortable. How impractical is that? Besides, I think you'll look kind of cute stuffed in there. I'll even put the top down if you'd like."

"It's thirty degrees outside!"

"What are you, chicken?"

"I don't care if you put the top down. It's not me that's going to look like I stuck my finger in an electrical outlet."

"After years of my own therapy, I'm finally at peace with the knowledge that my hair has a mind of its own.

"That's good that you're so comfortable with yourself. I would have figured you'd be much more self conscious about the dent in your chin."

Eve gasped in shock and brought her fingers to her chin. "I don't have a dent in my chin."

"Of course you don't," he said placatingly. "It was rude of me to bring it up. I'd only thought by your speech that you were comfortable with all your flaws."

"Well, I seem to be comfortable enough around you, so you're probably right. Get in the car. I'll make sure to make the trip as painless as possible," she said. The look in her eyes would have made Ruth proud.

Eve checked in with the front desk to let them know she had a guest before they made their way to the elevators and rode silently to the twenty-third floor where the WKTP offices were located.

"You're a little overdressed," Jake said, looking at the combination of jeans and sweats, Hawaiian shirts and spandex with amusement.

"Ahh…the joys of radio. That's why I love this job. This is my professional look. It's what people imagine I look like when they hear my voice, and I try to give them that image when I'm in public. Fortunately, I don't have to spend too much time in the public eye unless I'm teaching a class or doing a television appearance, and therefore, I keep my sanity. I'm perfectly content to sit behind the mic for the rest of my life."

"Well I have to say I like this image of you almost as much as your holy sweatpants look. You sure do have a pair of legs on you, Doc. Maybe next summer you can buy a pair of little shorts so I can ogle."

Eve didn't want to think about next summer. Of being without Jake. She locked the thought away when she heard the rapid clip-clop of heels, and knew the sound could only belong to one person.

"Here comes Lucy," she told Jake under her breath. "She's my producer, and she's been thinking about giving up her lesbian status ever since she heard your voice. Try not to make too much of an impression."

"I'll try to leave her heart intact," Jake said solemnly, putting his right hand up as if swearing in a court of law.

"How did the spot go over at the network?" Lucy asked, flipping through her clipboard, making notes and giving orders to an intern all at the same time.

"Great. We're going to do a commercial promoting the Christmas Eve show next week. It'll run the full week before Christmas."

"You also have a morning appearance on *Wake Up Dallas* next week and the *Good Morning America* spot the week after that, so you'll have to make sure all two of your business suits are dry cleaned," Lucy said sarcastically. The snicker from Eve's companion had her looking up, way up, into a pair of blue eyes that she could have drowned in.

"Shut up, Jake," Eve said, elbowing him in the ribs. "Lucy this is my good friend Jake Murphy. Jake, Lucy Porter."

"Ahh…Murphy-Madsen Construction. George did wonderful work on my condo several months ago," Lucy said, finally understanding why Eve only grinned every time she asked how the house was coming along.

"Nice to meet you, Lucy."

"Oh my God!" Lucy screamed, drawing everyone's attention. "You're *Waiting in Dallas*. I'd know that voice anywhere."

Eve winced at the announcement. She should have realized that Lucy would figure out who Jake was. Now she'd never hear the end of it.

"You've been holding out on me," Lucy accused. She turned her attention back to Jake. "You look even better than I imagined you would. You're a celebrity, you know?"

Jake couldn't keep the smile off his face. The woman was a steamroller. He figured she and Eve probably suited each other very well when working together.

"Thanks. I decided I wanted to see Eve work. I'm curious to see if she's as sexy in person when she spouts all of that advice as she is when I can only dream of her."

Eve rolled her eyes, but Lucy and Jake both ignored her.

"I've decided to like you," Lucy announced. "I'm a bitch for the most part, so this is a great honor I bestow upon you."

"I'll treasure it always," Jake assured her, straight faced.

"Come on. You can hang out in my office and watch the show through the glass wall. I'll be in the control panel, so you won't be in my way." Lucy took hold of his arm and dragged him away.

Jake looked over his shoulder in time to see Eve laughing by herself in the hallway. It was a good thing he'd had Ruth to get him used to crazy over the years because he was sure getting his fair share now with Eve in his life.

"*Anxious in Albuquerque*, you're on the air with Dr. Lovegood."

Jake watched her through the clear glass wall of Lucy's office and felt the wave of desire wash over him as soon as he heard the first words come across the airwaves. It was a feeling that was becoming much too familiar.

She'd taken her spiked heels off as soon as she sat in the oversized chair behind the control panel in the booth and propped a mile of long leg on a table that held something that looked suspiciously like donuts. No wonder he couldn't bribe her with them.

She hadn't paid him one bit of attention once she'd started her program two hours before. She had the ability to focus completely on whatever she was doing. He remembered her same intent focus when they made love, as if everything she did in everyday life was an experience to be savored. After what Steve Slater had done to her, he didn't blame her.

She fascinated him, and at the same time frustrated him so completely he didn't know how to handle her. She seemed to be perfectly content to go on exactly as they were, as if things were bound to end eventually and she was resigned to enjoying it while it lasted. He wanted marriage. A family. But every time he tried to approach the subject she cut him off. And broke his heart a little more.

She cared for him. He knew her well enough to know that she would never have taken him to her bed if she hadn't. She might even love him, not that she'd let him in on that little secret.

It all came down to trust. When all was said and done, she still felt like he'd eventually let her down. His past was stacked against him. After his time with Eve he couldn't remember the face of one of those women she was so sure he still wanted.

It was time to play hardball. He wanted to bring in the New Year with Eve Lovegood as his wife. He glanced at the phone on Lucy's desk and an idea began to form.

Eve tried to get Lucy's attention so she'd know she just handed her a caller without a title, but Lucy was involved in what looked like a heated discussion with one of the account executives so she would have to wing it.

It had taken every ounce of control she possessed for her to keep her eyes off Jake and listen to a never ending line of callers. She could feel the heat of his gaze on her with every movement she made, but she kept her head down and her nose buried in the paperwork in front of her.

"Thanks for calling in. You're on the air with Dr. Lovegood."

"Hey, Doc."

Eve's head snapped up and she caught Jake's clear blue gaze through the thin glass wall that separated them. The phone was pressed to his ear and his eyes were filled with desire. For her.

"Ahhh…*Waiting in Dallas.* I wondered when you'd call in."

She didn't notice that her voice had gotten huskier, but Jake did. Their eyes were locked and the game would be played, no matter what the consequences.

"Surely you're not still having problems with your love life. I thought we'd already worked out all the…kinks," she purred.

Jake nearly dropped the phone and said to hell with the charade. He didn't care who was listening. He wanted her.

"Oh, I think the kinks have been worked out just fine."

"That sounds promising, but I won't ask for the details since we have an audience. And your one true love? How is she faring? Or have you finally come to realize that it was only lust at first sight after all."

"I think she's. . .satisfied." He let the word trail off his lips like a caress.

Eve stopped the moan before it could escape, but the palpable silence over the airwaves crackled with tension.

"Bragging?" she asked.

"Never. Just honest. And my one true love has finally realized that I've been right all along."

"Right about what?"

"About it being love at first sight. She's loved me from the start. She was only afraid to admit it. But I'm a patient man. And I'll wait for the words I've needed to hear."

"You sound very sure of yourself."

"I have reason to believe that things will work out beautifully. I've waited my whole life for this woman, and I can't say she's made it easy for me. She's still not making it easy for me. But I'll get what I want in the end."

"That sounds like a challenge," Eve said, raising her eyebrow. She met his gaze without flinching.

"It *is* a challenge," he said smirking back at her. "But the ball is in her court now. What do you think about dinner?" he asked, succeeding at throwing her off course.

"What about dinner?" Eve didn't know how she'd lost control of the conversation. He made it seem like she was the one that was being difficult when in reality he was the one that changed women like days of the week underpants. She'd have to be a complete imbecile to drop her well constructed armor for Jake Murphy when she'd barely survived her time with Steve Slater. She knew the difference between them. Steve had never been half the man that Jake was, but he was still a man.

"I was thinking she'd like to have a late dinner somewhere quiet, somewhere where she can tell me what I need to hear," Jake said, seeing her frustration, at herself, at him. "And then I thought I'd make love to her until she realizes I could never want another woman the way I want her."

Eve's throat was as dry as dust. "What woman wouldn't want that? It sounds like she's lucky to have you." Her eyes never left his and her gaze was full of tenderness. Of Love. It was only the two of them in the building, the thin glass wall wasn't between them and there weren't a million people listening as she lost the best part of herself to a man she wasn't sure wouldn't end up leaving her heart in pieces.

The late night drive from the station was made in comfortable silence. Eve had willingly given Jake the keys when he'd held out his hand for them as they'd left the building. Her mind was crowded with thoughts—restless—and nerves made it difficult for the tension to seep out of her shoulders.

The night was cold, freezing, and flurries turned to wet mush as they landed on the ground. Jake handled the car with ease despite the difficulty he'd had with fitting his large frame inside. The heat was turned on low and the wipers swished hypnotically, but she still found it difficult for her thoughts to settle. She loved him. Why were the words so much harder than the act itself?

She studied his profile. Intelligent eyes in the face of a warrior, a stubborn chin and a grin that could melt the hardest of hearts.

"If you keep staring at me like that, I'm going to have to pull the car over and take advantage of you."

"I love you," Eve blurted out. She felt as if a freight train had landed on her chest and she was having a little trouble breathing.

"I know," Jake said, pulling the car to the side of the road, "but it's nice to hear you say it."

"I think I'm going to be sick," Eve said, putting her head between her knees.

"This is not exactly how I imagined this moment," Jake said, laughing at the absurdity of it all.

"Eve, look at me." He lifted her chin, so her eyes met his. He could see the nerves, the fear, and through it all, the love. "I love you, too." He kissed her gently. "See, that wasn't so bad."

"Yeah, piece of cake."

He chuckled at the dry tone of her voice. "Now sit back and relax. This is a night I'll want you to remember."

"I'd think it would be pretty hard to forget.

Where are we?" Eve asked, realizing they were headed in the opposite direction of her house.

"I told you. We're going to have a late dinner, and then I'm going to take you home and make love to you until exhaustion sets in."

Home. It seemed her home was with Jake.

"That sounds wonderful. I'm starving," she smiled, a feminine smile full of mystery and promise.

Jake nearly swallowed his tongue and put his foot down on the gas pedal. Maybe they'd stop at a drive-through instead.

chapter fourteen

The ringing of the doorbell halted Eve's path to the kitchen for more desperately needed coffee. Jake had been true to his word, she thought with a smile. She'd gotten very little sleep the night before, and now she was reduced to daydreaming and a caffeine addiction.

The doorbell rang again before she was to the door.

"Coming," she called out.

She was glad she'd done away with the original screeching cat doorbell that she was told was the original from when the house was built. Original or not, it hurt her ears and frightened every animal in the neighborhood. She was perfectly content with the soft tones of a Major third.

"Detective Rosenberg," Eve said, surprised.

"If I could take a few minutes of your time, Dr. Lovegood, I'd appreciate it."

"Of course. Please come in. I was just about to make fresh coffee. You'll join me?"

"Yes, thank you."

Eve almost laughed at the desperate look he got in his eyes when she mentioned coffee. Poor guy must not get a decent cup very often. She moved around the kitchen easily, though she was less than competent in the space, and set cups and saucers on the table as well as the coffee cake that Gretchen had left from her baking the day before.

"Do you have any leads on who caused the explosion?" Eve asked, sitting across from him.

The kitchen door opened before he could answer her, and Jake walked in. They'd started work on the carriage house and gazebo earlier in the week, so he spent most of his days alternating between there and his office. Since George was the one that did most of the hands-on work, Jake was more often seen in a suit and tie meeting with clients than he was in jeans and flannel shirts like he was today. Eve couldn't decide which one she liked him in more.

"Detective," Jake acknowledged, nodding his head and heading over to the sink to wash his hands. "I saw you pull up and thought you might have news."

"Yes, I do. I was just about to tell Dr. Lovegood that we've caught the man responsible for the explosion. He also confessed to writing the notes and following her to and from work."

Eve's mouth fell open in surprise. This was the last thing she'd expected to hear. Jake came up behind her and put a comforting hand on her shoulder. She could tell by the pressure of his fingers that he was just as surprised as she was.

"How did you catch him? Who was he?" Eve asked.

"We followed the news," he said vaguely. Before Eve could ask more questions he jumped in with the details. "We noticed a series of articles about you and your husband over an extended amount of time. Most of them weren't very flattering to you and seem to speculate heavily on your relationship. The articles seemed personal and not at all newsworthy."

"So you're saying a reporter caused all this so he'd have a story?"

"That seems to be the case. He thought a story about America's favorite love doctor being stalked by a psychopath would make good copy, but he said you didn't give him the reaction he was hoping for since you had a man around the house. The explosion was simply to get your face and the story of your marriage back on page one of the paper. It seems he was a big fan of Steve Slater's."

"Most people were," she said, her face blank. Jake rubbed the tension from her shoulders and she leaned her head back against him. The more she was with Jake, the less her past seemed to matter. She was healing.

"Well, the man's behind bars and I doubt he'll be able to find a job for another newspaper after this stunt. I just wanted to let you know," he said, draining his cup of every drop of coffee and shrugging into his coat. "We won't need you to testify since he made a full confession, but you will need to sign a statement that verifies his confession."

"Yes," Eve said, shaking herself back to reality and seeing the detective to the door. "I'll do that."

"Thanks for the coffee."

Eve shut the door behind him and turned into Jake when he put his arms around her. "It almost seems as if it were all a dream," she said, burrowing into his scent, a combination of soap, aftershave and sweat.

"It's over now. I thought you'd still be sleeping."

"I made myself crawl out of bed. I didn't think your ego needed another boost. How is it you can still look good after that little sleep?"

"I have good genes. What can I say?"

"Speaking of Ruth…"

"Were we?" Jake asked, kissing her forehead and backing her towards the room they'd been sharing.

Her brain immediately went foggy at the first touch of his lips.

"You were saying." He pulled the covers back on the bed and nudged her down easily. The protest she made in the back of her throat when he didn't follow her down made him smile.

"I have a week off before the Christmas Eve show. I thought I'd take Ruth Christmas shopping. I know exactly what I want to get you."

"She'd like that," he said kissing her once more. She was addictive, more than any drug. He thought of the ring he had locked in the safe in his office and knew it didn't matter what Eve gave him for Christmas. Nothing could be more precious than the gift of her love. Now all he had to do was talk her into marriage.

He watched as sleep claimed her.

chapter fifteen

The unusual cold weather they'd received the first two weeks of December disappeared by week three. It was sixty degrees and noses sniffled and forecasters shook their heads at the fickleness of Texas weather.

The ring was burning a hole in his pocket. Jake lifted the lid of the little velvet box and stared at the shimmering stone with pride. She would wear his symbol of love for the rest of their lives, and even then the diamond would last for generations.

He looked around the house he'd come to think of as his own. Blood, sweat and a few tears that he'd never admit to had gone into a home that he and Eve would share. Raise their children in. The house needed love, laughter and little feet pounding up and down the stairs.

He planned to propose Christmas Eve. The scene was set in his head. The hearth would be lit and the tree lights would be ablaze. There'd be wine and he'd make love with her on the rug in front of the fireplace.

The slam of a car door had him snapping the lid of the box closed and shoving it in his pocket. He looked at his watch and figured it was Ruth and Eve returning from their shopping trip. His grandmother had been thrilled at the idea of getting some shopping done, but if he knew his grandmother, and he did, he also knew that Eve would probably need a large glass of wine after the excursion.

He headed out the kitchen door, assuming they'd need help with the heaps of shopping bags he was sure Eve had in her trunk, and stopped dead in his tracks. It wasn't Ruth and Eve, but someone from his past. Someone that had always held part of his heart.

"Melissa?" Jake asked in surprise, a grin splitting his face.

"Don't tell me you don't recognize me," she said with a pout. "It hasn't been that long. I stopped by your house, but I was told you've been residing here," she said with a raised eyebrow. "I think you have some explaining to do."

She rested against the hood of her car, aware of

the picture she made since posing was her career—
a stunning blonde with eyes blue as the ocean in a
winter white cowl-necked dress that stopped at mid
calf. A black belt rested at her hips and knee high
black leather boots added an extra three inches to
her already substantial height. She was glad to be
away from New York, from the cameras and
makeup artists. She looked at the man she'd loved
her entire life and smiled. She was eight years
younger, and he was still the only man she'd ever let
into her heart.

"I can see you're still quite the
conversationalist," she said, twin dimples making an
appearance. "Don't you at least have a hug for your
favorite cousin?"

Jake leaped across the yard with a war whoop
and swooped her into a spinning circle while
hugging her close.

"It's been a long time since I've been shopping with
someone that could keep up with me," Ruth said,
leaning her seat back in the Miata. "I could still go
for hours."

Eve thought of aching feet and begged God for
mercy. She'd been exhausted after the first four
hours. Ruth was an indescribable force of energy

that could be bottled and sold for a fortune.

"You're not tired, are you, girl?"

"Nope, I could go for hours," Eve lied with a straight face.

"Good. I want you to have plenty of energy to seduce my grandson tonight. I would never want it to be said that I came between a woman who was trying to get in her man's pants."

"Umm…"

"Stop all those blushes. You'd think you'd be over all that by now, especially since you talk about sex in front of millions of people every day. What's wrong with a little gossip between women after all that?"

"Nothing," Eve said, smiling. "Nothing at all." She thought of the puppy that she'd bought for Jake, a Golden Retriever that would be eight weeks old Christmas day. She'd give him his childhood.

"Now, about my great-grandbabies," Ruth began, but Eve's attention was on her house. Actually it was on Jake and the woman he was holding onto like she held the secret of life in her cleavage. She went numb as she parked the car and got out slowly.

Ruth came around to stand beside her, but Eve didn't see the smile on her face, she was too busy waiting for Jake to notice her presence.

"Would you look at those breasts?" Ruth said,

nudging Eve in the ribs. "I've been thinking about buying myself a pair, but I hear they're dreadfully expensive."

Eve carefully blanked her face when Jake looked up and caught her stare. His arm stayed around the woman, and Eve could tell he was only half listening as the woman babbled on. The look he gave her told her nothing. There was no guilt on his face, but it looked something closer along the lines of hurt. She was the one who was hurt. She'd loved him. She still loved him, even after this betrayal. He wouldn't get a reaction out of her, and she wouldn't tell herself "I told you so," no matter how tempting it was.

"Eve," Ruth said, with another nudge. "Did you hear what I said?"

"Yes," she answered, mechanically.

"It's a shame hers are real. Some women have all the luck."

"You know her?" Eve asked, curious.

"Of course I know her. She's my granddaughter. But she didn't get those puppies from my side of the family. No sir."

Eve felt shame wash over her and snapped her head back to Jake, but his expression was as blank as hers had been a moment ago.

"Let's go see how long she's here for. You'll like her, Eve. Jake practically raised her since her parents took lessons from Jake's on how to abandon your only child. I should have beaten my boys more when they were younger, but I made up for it by raising two amazing grandchildren."

Ruth pulled Eve along behind her with enough force that she had no choice but to follow or be dragged. The kitchen was warm, and Gretchen had left plenty of food to be eaten for dinner, but the cold that had invaded her body ever since she'd pulled up to the house hadn't left her.

Jake's introduction of Melissa was stilted and formal, and he didn't greet her with his usual kiss. The air was ripe with tension, but Ruth and Melissa didn't seem to feel it as they caught up on things.

"Eve dear, you're looking a little pale," Ruth remarked. "It looks like you couldn't keep up with me after all. You should have told me when you got too tired. I have a tendency to get blinders on when I see a shoe sale."

"No, I'm fine," Eve protested. "But I think I will go lie down for a while. I'm glad to have met you, Melissa. You're welcome to stay for as long as you'd like. There's a guest room next door to Ruth's if you'd like, or you can take your pick of rooms on the upper floors."

"What about the tower room?" Melissa asked excitedly.

She was so young, Eve thought with a smile.

Not much younger than Eve in years, but in innocence they were lifetimes apart.

"The west tower is my office," she said, "but the east tower is a small bedroom."

"Sold," she said with a laugh.

Eve smiled in return at the girl's exuberance. She couldn't help but respond to someone so honest and open. But reality crashed back with a bang when she caught Jake's stare. She slipped out of the room and up the stairs to her bedroom, the room they had loved in just the night before. Why did it seem like a lifetime ago?

She stiffened when she felt his presence behind her, but she deliberately made herself relax.

"I'm sorry, Jake," she said, turning to face him, so he'd know that she knew she'd been wrong not to trust him.

"Sorry's not good enough, Eve." His face was unforgiving—hurt and angry.

"I made a mistake," she said, her own hurt coming to the surface. Anger was the only way she knew how to deal with it effectively. "I've apologized, but the evidence was pretty damning when I drove up. What was I supposed to think? You haven't exactly had the best track record when it comes to women."

"You were supposed to trust me. Period. It's what I would have done because love and trust go hand in hand. You haven't figured that out yet," he said, throwing his hands up in frustration. "You say you love me, but I don't think you know how to love. You're so caught up in the absurdity of a marriage you despised to look to the future, to see what real love is."

He swore at himself as he watched the color drain from her face. "I'm not him, Eve. And you're not the same person you were when you married him, though you're trying damned hard to hold on to her. I love you, but we have nothing until you can figure out what you want for yourself. I won't stand by and listen to your declarations of love when you doubt who I am as a man."

She didn't break down until he closed the door quietly behind him. Her chest was crushed by an invisible weight and just breathing was a labor in itself. She dropped to her knees on the floor and curled into herself when the tears started to fall.

chapter sixteen

Eve did her best to go downstairs as if nothing was wrong. Her eyes were gritty and swollen from the tears she'd shed, and her heart felt as if a piece was missing since Jake hadn't slept in the house the night before. She'd gotten so used to him being there that it felt empty now that he was gone.

She almost went back upstairs when she saw Melissa in the kitchen. She didn't feel like being social, no matter how nice the woman was.

"Good morning," Melissa said, automatically pouring a second cup of coffee for Eve while she was up. She'd noticed Eve's swollen eyes the moment she'd walked into the room, and the look of devastation on her face was so heartbreaking that she wanted to do nothing but comfort the woman.

Men. They did nothing but cause trouble, she thought. Even if the man in question was her own cousin. It was exactly why she was going to focus on her career and stay as far away as possible from the species.

Jake was an idiot she'd decided the night before. She would have thought the same things that had gone through Eve's head if she'd seen the man she loved holding onto a strange woman as familiarly as Jake had been holding her. She'd told him so too the night before when he'd so stubbornly walked away from a woman he was obviously head over heels in love with.

Melissa brought Eve the coffee and set down across from her. "Jake said he's going to be away for a while. He's got some loose ends to tie up before he can take off for the holidays." She felt satisfaction as Eve's spoon clattered against the side of her cup at the mention of Jake's name.

"That's fine," Eve said as though the thought of being without him for the rest of the week, much less forever, didn't faze her a bit.

"I want you to know that I think Jake's an idiot," Melissa said, taking Eve's hand. "I told him so."

The sympathy she saw in Melissa's gaze was almost Eve's undoing, but she kept the tears at bay. "No, he was right to be angry. I didn't trust him, and if I'm going to love him I have to trust him, no matter what the circumstances."

"That's phooey," Melissa said.

"Phooey?" Eve asked.

"Gran bet me a thousand dollars I couldn't stop cussing. I'm a master at it. I'm told it's a lost art to be able to do it properly, but it's Gran's fault I started in the first place. I never would have heard those words to begin with if she hadn't taken me to the horse races when I was thirteen. I thought Jake was going to strangle her for exposing me to something like that."

Eve smiled with her and thought it was sad that Jake had been the one to be concerned for the child when her parents hadn't bothered.

"Anyway, it's not like Jake bent over backwards to give you the right impression of our relationship. He's just as much at fault as you are. He expects unwavering trust, but there's only so far that can take you before you have to start explaining yourself."

Eve felt lighter at the woman's words. Jake should have never doubted her love for him. Everybody makes mistakes, especially in relationships. She should know that better than anyone.

"I just wanted you to know that I gave Jake hell last night before he left. Someone needed to be in your corner, and Gran was out of commission because she drank a few hot toddies to ease the ache in her feet, but I always thought hot toddies were for colds, so I'm not sure if that was the truth or not. I think she probably just wanted to get drunk without us griping at her."

"Are you allowed to say hell?" Eve asked, getting the hang of Melissa's constant change of topics and unusual thoughts. She was definitely Ruth's granddaughter.

"Hell is a place," Melissa replied. "It would hardly seem fair if I couldn't talk about a location now would it?"

"No, I suppose not."

"Now tell me how you're going to make Jake suffer."

"I'm not going to make him suffer. I was just as much at fault as he was, and something I've learned in my line of work is that sometimes you have to swallow your pride. I'm going to enjoy my week off even if it kills me and hope that he's just as miserable. And if that doesn't work, I'm going to get down on my knees and beg for forgiveness."

"That ought to teach him," Melissa said, tipping her coffee cup in a salute to the oddities of love.

Jake was more than miserable. There wasn't a word

to describe exactly what he was feeling—he just knew it wasn't good.

The inside of his mouth felt like sandpaper and his head was no longer attached to his body. His own grandmother had turned against him and decided he didn't deserve to live.

It had taken less than twenty-four hours for him to get loose ends tied up for the business and less than twelve to realize he'd been an idiot to leave Eve. He'd stood outside her room for what seemed like hours and listened to the heart wrenching sobs from the other side of the door. He'd felt like the lowest kind of life form, but he'd left her anyway only to run into Melissa's sharp tongue on the way out.

His house was to be his refuge, but then Ruth had shown up on the pretense of missing Edward. She'd just happened to have two bottles of Jameson's in her handbag. She'd told him in no uncertain terms that a Murphy that couldn't handle his alcohol was no blood kin of hers, so he, Ruth and Edward made their way through both bottles. Though now that he thought about it, Ruth and Edward had seemed perfectly fine when they'd gotten up to find their beds.

The smell of meat from the kitchen and rattling pots and pans did equal justice to his stomach and his head.

"Are you going to sleep all day, Jake? It was just a little whiskey," Ruth said, opening the drapes in the living room so bright sunlight hit him right in the face. The scream that came from his lips made Ruth chuckle. Jake closed his eyes and wished for death. And then he wished for Eve. If he hadn't been so stupid this would have never happened.

"I hope you've learned your lesson, young man," Ruth said, putting her face less than two inches from his own and scaring the hell out of him when he opened his eyes. "Relationships don't work if one partner only takes and the other only gives. Listen to your Gran, honey. I didn't bury six husbands without learning a little. How are you supposed to make babies when you're miles apart?"

Jake groaned and turned his head slowly away from the light and his grandmother. Not even sex sounded good to him right now, that's what sorry shape he was in.

"Of course," she went on like he hadn't just dismissed her, "Eve's a beautiful woman. There are probably plenty of men that would be glad to take your place. Edward has a grandson that's just Eve's age who sells insurance. He's very nice," Ruth said, sitting on the floor Indian style in front of the coffee table and waiting for Edward to set her breakfast down.

"Please join us, Edward," Ruth commanded

before he could leave again. "Jake your breakfast is getting cold."

Jake growled at the thought of Eve with anyone but him and then groaned as the smell of food overpowered him. He used what little strength he had to run to the bathroom before he disgraced himself, and he used the last of it to curse his grandmother.

It wasn't until after he'd showered and gotten dressed, planning how he could throw himself on Eve's mercy and beg for forgiveness when he found out she'd gone to spend a few days with her family.

She'd left him.

chapter seventeen

Eve felt better than she had in a long time. The visit with her family had been exactly what she needed. Her mother had welcomed her with a hug and then demanded to know what the hell was going on, and if she was still in love with the man who'd been seducing her with his words over the radio. Trust her mother to always cut straight to the heart of the matter.

She'd vented her frustrations and fears, assured her mother that she loved Jake with all her heart, and then promptly received a verbal kick in the pants for running away from her problems instead of facing them head on. There was nothing like family to bring you back down to earth.

She'd gone by the house to drop off her bags and see how her house guests were faring. Ruth and Melissa had decided to stay on and look after the place while she was away. Melissa told her she was staying so that she didn't miss anything exciting if Jake happened to stop by, which was almost exactly what Ruth had told her not ten minutes before in another room.

Eve was comfortably dressed in black sweatpants and a gaudy red sweatshirt with real Christmas lights that blinked on and off and a picture of a giant Santa head in the middle. It was time for her favorite show of the year, and her hands only shook a little when she opened the door to the studio. She was almost to the point where she didn't think about the phone call she'd received five years ago to the day. Almost.

A pitiful Christmas tree stood in the hallway between the elevators and the control center, and the booth was lit with dozens of sparkling lights. There were cookies set out cut in the shape of erotic elves and dipped in green and red sugar crystals. It wasn't such a bad place to spend Christmas Eve.

"Have some eggnog," Lucy offered, as Eve waited for the booth to be clear so she could go in.

In Eve's opinion, it looked as if Lucy had been hitting the Eggnog all day. "Are you all right, Lucy?"

"Never been better," Lucy chirped with a

crooked smile. "I've got a copy of your program, and there are plenty of people to screen calls. It will be a great show, just like always."

Eve put her hand on Lucy's shoulder lightly and watched as the woman before her crumpled like a rag doll. "Suzanne said she needed some space, and the house-hunting was making things a little too serious," Lucy said, sniffling.

"Oh, Lucy. I'm sorry. It's been a hell of a week, hasn't it? I haven't done so hot in the love department either. You're welcome to spend Christmas with me."

"No, I'm leaving tonight to get to my folks place. I should be there in time to open gifts in the morning. My brothers and their families will all be there, just like every year."

She straightened her shoulders and dashed the tears away. Sometimes Lucy was too tough for her own good.

"Well, maybe you can stop by for New Year's," Eve said, already planning an impromptu party. "I'd love for you to see the house."

"Can I get drunk?"

"Absolutely," Eve said, laughing.

"I'll be there," Lucy said, returning her smile. "Now let's get this show on the road.

Eve entered the booth with her notes and a bottle of water, just like she did every night she was on the air, and felt her confidence slip with every minute that passed bringing her closer to air time. She knew what she had to do, but no one said it would be easy.

She listened to the music that led to her intro and wiped her damp hands on her sweatpants. "Merry Christmas," she said. "This is Dr. Eve Lovegood coming to you with a four hour Christmas Eve special. I hope you're having a joyful holiday season, whether you're spending it with family or friends, a lover or on your own. Christmas is a season that makes us think about what we have or don't have in our lives, what we want versus what we need. And when you're with someone you love, the season only becomes sweeter. On the other hand, if it's a time when you've experienced loss, nothing can make this particular holiday seem more painful."

Eve looked at Lucy through the glass to her office, saw the woman take another drink of eggnog and knew, from her own experience, she spoke nothing less than the truth.

"Before I tackle the subject of love and loss around the holidays, and before I take your calls, I'd like to take a minute to talk about something personal. I think sometimes you as listeners don't realize that I face the same problems you do. That I sit in this booth and hand out advice based on what

I learned from the different degrees that hang on my wall. But I want to tell you that I struggle the same as everyone else when it comes to relationships. The heart is not logical but emotional, which is why my degrees are meaningless when it comes to my own troubles."

The roiling was fierce in her stomach, but she forged ahead.

"Most of you have followed the caller known only to you as *Waiting in Dallas*. I won't tell you his name, but I will tell you that I love him very much. We met by chance, as the fates often deem when it comes to something as intangible as love, and he told me, and you," she added, "that he fell in love with me the first moment he laid eyes on me."

Eve laughed into the microphone. "It wasn't so clear cut to a hardened cynic such as me, but I eventually realized I was in love with him too. And then, as is the way of relationships, things got complicated. I don't ever talk about my past, but I feel it's important to a certain extent to reveal a few things about myself. I had a horrible first marriage. It didn't start out that way. It was a whirlwind of things that young girls in love always imagine. And then reality found us. My first marriage was abusive to the point where I didn't really know who the person Eve Lovegood was anymore. *Doctor* Lovegood was always much easier to know, you see. My first marriage taught me that love is much easier to give than trust. And once the trust is broken, the love is not far behind.

"I made a mistake with *Waiting in Dallas*. The love was there, but I wasn't willing to trust him. Mostly because of what my marriage did to me, but also because I was just afraid to put a part of myself in someone else's hands and wonder if they were going to nurture what I had given them or crush it to dust.

"So I want to say to you and to him, that I was wrong. I love you *Waiting in Dallas*, and I trust you with my heart, whatever you want to do with it. It's yours. And I hope that it's not too late for me to hold onto yours."

Eve made it through her notes on her original topic as if it were a typical show, and the nerves didn't resurface until she opened the phone lines. She waited for him to call. She wanted him to call, but midnight came around with no call from *Waiting in Dallas*.

"We haven't done so hot, huh, kid?" Lucy asked, walking out to the parking garage with Eve. It was officially Christmas morning, and Eve couldn't think of anything more depressing.

"Nope. I figured I'd celebrate the season by opening a bottle of Dom Perignon I've been saving for a special occasion, putting on a slinky negligee and turning on my Bing Crosby Christmas CD."

"Not a bad idea," Lucy said, getting into her bright red Saab. "I'll keep that in mind for next year."

"Drive safe," Eve said, waving goodbye and slipping into her own car. Miatas weren't the ideal car for winter weather. Maybe she should think about getting something a little larger. She automatically thought of Jake's long legs cramped into a little space and shrugged away the thought. He hadn't called. She had to remember that.

The city was quiet and still. There was hardly any traffic on the wide streets. She turned the heater up higher and snuggled into her wool coat for the drive home. The warm temperature had only lasted a few days before getting cold again, and already snow flurries were falling against her windshield and on the roads to make mush.

When she turned onto her street, Christmas lights were still blazing from one house to the next. Her house stood dark at the end of the cul-de-sac, only the soft glow from her tree in the living room showed that she had any Christmas spirit at all.

Eve assumed Melissa and Ruth had gone to Jake's to celebrate together despite their proclamations of women sticking together. In the end, blood was thicker than water. She parked in front of the house instead of pulling to the back like she usually did and stood in the cold for a few minutes, the peace of the night surrounding her and numbing the pain in her heart.

She'd made the decision on her way home. She'd put the house on the market after the first of the year. It had to be done. She couldn't keep living here with memories of Jake around every corner.

She dug to the bottom of her bag and walked up the stairs to her front door. It hadn't been so long ago when Jake had first knocked down her door. The warmth that greeted her was more than welcome, and she shrugged out of her long coat and scarf and hung them both on the coat rack beside the front door.

The house was still around her, and she realized it was the first time since she'd moved in that there had been complete silence in the large space. Maybe she'd forgo the wine and CDs. Bed was sounding better and better after the night she'd had.

The sight of the fire crackling in the hearth stopped her. It hadn't been lit when she'd left and surely Ruth and Melissa knew not to leave it unattended when no one was home. She guessed she should be thankful the house was still standing.

The gasp that left her was quickly contained as she looked closer at the scene. A bottle of champagne was being iced in a bucket and two crystal flutes sat next to it. There were roses everywhere. Dozens. Red and full, the scent was fragrant and sweet. Tears came to her eyes before she could control it.

"I would have had a glass ready for you, but I wasn't sure what time you'd get in."

Eve whirled around at the voice behind her and laughed as she got sight of him. He was in grey sweats and wore a tacky sweatshirt similar to her own. He looked amazing, like an oasis in the desert after the week they'd spent apart. And to her embarrassment the tears wouldn't stop.

"I waited for you to call," she said when he didn't come to her.

She was caught in the rabbit hole and didn't know how to get out, and her cheeks heated at the slip that she'd wanted to hear his voice.

"I thought this deserved some privacy," he said. "I wanted to call in, but I wasn't sure my voice would work after the things you said. I owe you an apology."

"No, you don't. You were right. I didn't trust you enough."

"Maybe not, but I certainly never did anything to help reassure you that my actions were warranted. I asked you for something without giving you proof that you could trust me. Will you come with me?" he asked, holding out his hand.

Eve put her hand in his and felt the shock that

ran up her arm from a simple touch. "I've missed you."

"I was just thinking the same thing," he said, leading her to the fireplace. He popped the cork on the champagne and poured two glasses, handing one to Eve.

"I don't think I can wait to do this any longer," he said bringing his mouth to hers. The kiss was just as potent as their first, full of desire and promises, only now Eve was able to recognize them for what they were.

"I've dreamed about you and ached for you at night," he said, smoothing the hair back from her face in a gentle gesture—a gesture she'd gotten used to over the past months. "And I want to give you a new Christmas memory. A happy memory. I love you, Eve. More than I did at the beginning, and tomorrow it will be more than today. Spend your life with me. Marry me."

Eve buried her head in his neck and wept away the unnecessary pain they'd caused each other over the past week. "I love you so much," she said, kissing him with desperation.

"Is that a yes?" he asked, his heart in his gaze. He pulled the diamond he'd been carrying for weeks out of his pocket and slipped it on to her finger. "It looks just right there."

"It's perfect," Eve said. "Yes, I'll marry you."

She looked at the brilliant gem flash in the firelight and knew true happiness. "I want children," she said out of the blue, causing Jake to pause in his kissing.

"Right now?" he asked.

"Well, your grandmother does want a great-grandchild by next Christmas."

"Oh, well then, I guess we'd better get started."

He lowered her to the rug in front of the fireplace and proceeded to do just that.

epilogue

A Year Later…

"An old woman asks for one simple request," Ruth complained, "and you can't even come through. This could be my last Christmas, you know?"

Melissa stifled a laugh at the mutinous expression on her grandmother's face. "You don't ask for much, Gran. You're such an easy person to please."

"Shut up, brat. Don't think that I'm pleased that you've come to another holiday without a husband in tow. You're not getting any younger you know."

"I've decided I'm never getting married," Melissa said with a mischievous glint in her eyes. "I'm just going to have dozens of affairs with dashing

191

Counts and Greek gods just like my granny taught me."

"Stop teasing, Melissa," Jake said laughing. He turned his attention to Ruth. "It serves you right for meddling in other people's business. Besides, some things don't happen on your time table. You'll have your great-grandson by New Year's." He rubbed his hand gently over Eve's swollen belly and felt a thrill at the impatient movement beneath. "It's a late Christmas present, but I don't even think you can complain about that, Gran."

He smiled at Eve and noticed the immediate flash of pain in her eyes. "What's wrong?" he demanded.

When Eve began laughing uncontrollably he started to get really worried. "Eve, tell me what's wrong. Is it the baby?"

"I think your grandmother might be right," she said. "I think this baby's going to be born on Christmas after all," she said, grimacing through another contraction.

"God knows to listen to people as old as I am," Ruth said, grabbing her handbag and directing Melissa to Eve's suitcase in the closet. "At my age, I'm practically His right hand man."

Ruth closed the door behind them and crowded into the back seat of the SUV that Jake had bought after he'd found out Eve was pregnant.

She decided not to tell them that she prayed all the way to the hospital and through the next twelve hours of sitting in a waiting room. There were some secrets a woman her age needed to keep, but when she held her great-grandson in her arms for the first time, she knew that heaven couldn't get much better than this.

about the author

Liliana Hart is the New York Times and USA Today bestselling author of more than a thirty books. She lives in Texas in a big rambling house with her laptop and cats, and she spends way too much time on Twitter. She loves hearing from her readers.

19123856R00113

Printed in Great Britain
by Amazon